CALLUNA

SPELL LIBRARY BOOK 4

JEWELS ARTHUR

This is a work of fiction. Names, characters, places, and incidents either are the product of the author's imagination or are used fictitiously. Any resemblance to actual persons, living or dead, events, or locales is entirely coincidental.

Copyright © 2020 by Jewels Arthur
Calluna

All rights reserved. No part of this book may be reproduced or used in any manner without written permission of the copyright owner except for the use of quotations in a book review. For more information, address: jewelsarthur@gmail.com.

Book design by: Josie Cluney
Editing/Proofreading by: Bookish Dreams Editing & Lucy Felthouse
Formatting by: Inked Imagination

Published by Jewels Arthur

ISBN 9798648962972 (paperback)
ASIN B086GFHRZJ (ebook)

Dedication

To Kyle and Charlotte, you both are the best. I love you more than you will ever know. To the farthest planet and back. Wubba lubba dub dub.

To my Silver Springs Library ladies, ya'll are the best and I am privileged to be able to work with every single one of you.

To my Wampitch and Vampire, you guys are so amazing. Thank you for dealing with this mermaid.

Thank you to my amazing PA Sarah Klinger. Love you girl, thanks for keeping me sane.

To my alpha readers, Jenni, Mollie, Sam, Rachel, Sherry, Daisy, Janet, Robin, and Voe.
You are all amazing and I am so lucky to have you guys on my team.

CONTENTS

1. Calluna — 1
2. Calluna — 5
3. Calluna — 9
4. Calluna — 14
5. Calluna — 19
6. Landyn — 25
7. Calluna — 29
8. Rhett — 34
9. Calluna — 39
10. Calluna — 44
11. Calluna — 48
12. Landyn — 52
13. Calluna — 56
14. Rhett — 60
15. Calluna — 65
16. Calluna — 70
17. Damian — 76
18. Calluna — 82
19. Calluna — 89
20. Calluna — 95
21. Landyn — 99
22. Calluna — 103
23. Rhett — 108
24. Calluna — 113
25. Landyn — 120
26. Calluna — 124
27. Calluna — 129
28. Damian — 133
29. Calluna — 140
30. Elias — 145
31. Calluna — 152
32. Calluna — 156

33. Calluna	163
34. Calluna	168
35. Calluna	173
36. Calluna	178
37. Calluna	183
38. Calluna	187
Epilogue	195
Dahlia by Tabitha Barret	203
Chapter 1	205
Spell Library Books	209
To The Reader:	211
Also by Jewels Arthur	213
About the Author	215
Follow Jewels Arthur on Social Media	217

Chapter 1

Calluna

"I have never seen something so rashy." I pause, grimacing at the sight. "Or long, for that matter."

"He is extremely long for his age," Lars agrees, stroking along Klaus' length. "He is so soft."

"He should be, I just washed him," I add with a smile, watching Lars cuddle up with Klaus. "I really hope he gets adopted soon. He was in bad shape when he got here, but I'm hoping the rash is the last trace of this curse."

Lars, my one and only worker, nods his head. "What kind of monster would curse a ferret?" He growls the words, and the rumble they make in his chest makes me bite my lip. *Fuck, I need to get laid.*

"Stop looking at me like that," Lars growls again, quirking his brow at me. "You really need to get laid. You should have seen the guy I hooked up with last night. You'd be biting that lip off."

"Why do you have to be gay? Why do you have to get laid so much more than I do?" I moan, stealing Klaus from his grasp. This is what I get for having a very sexy but perpetually unavailable best friend. His long, sandy blond hair is slicked back on the top and shaved tightly on the sides. A medium-length grizzled beard frames a square jaw and full lips. Pure sexual goodness all wrapped up in a gay best friend package. Isn't that my luck? His body literally brings new meaning to the disgusting phrase I hear kids using these days—*cum gutters*.

Lars looks at me seriously, losing his charming smile. "Because I leave this place every once in a while, and go somewhere other than back to my apartment. I'm gay because cock is amazing and pussy freaks me out."

I purse my lips and continue to pet Klaus' soft fur. I am definitely in need of a good lay if I am this turned on by my very gay best friend, even if he is super hunky. He does have this all right though. All sex and no strings. That is where it's at.

"Come to Vee with me tonight. We'll have a blast, dance all night, find something stiff, long, and definitely not rashy." He jabs me in the side, causing me to laugh loudly and Klaus to leap from my hands. He runs over to the other side of the store where we keep the pet beds and crawls into them, hiding from the loud noise.

"What kind of man am I going to find at Vee? The only attractive ones are the owners, and Rose locked down those guys months ago."

"We're just looking for a bit of fun, not a husband. A good fuck with some random, and then onto a morning of nursing a hangover and a sore pussy," Lars replies with a grin.

I eye him skeptically. "First of all, I never said anything about a husband, and I don't want to be nursing a hangover."

"But you are fine with the sore pussy?" Lars jeers with a glint in his eye.

"Of course I am," I say without shame.

"So you'll go?" he asks hopefully, and I just shrug at him.

"Meh," I reply noncommittally. My living room, shitty TV, and relaxing in only a t-shirt and undies are calling my name.

I look down and see the corny romance book sitting on my table and roll my eyes. Someone left it in the store earlier today. It looks funny with all the half-naked guys and flowers, but it also looks like a silly love story and that is so not my scene. My biggest interest in the book though is that the author is from Silver Springs. Maybe reading the book will help me figure out who C. C. Pines is. Settling on reading it tonight, I look up to see Lars glaring at me.

"What?" I say through my teeth, squinting my eyes at him.

"I believe you have to pick the book up to read it. Unless you have powers that I don't know about?" he says with a laugh, causing my face to flush a bit. I hate that he saw my interest in the book, hate that it makes me look desperate. It's easier to convince people that I'm truly fine with being alone when I avoid all the gushy shit.

"I'm just trying to see if I can spot some man cock around the flowers. The guy on the right seems to be holding a pretty small bouquet," I point out, turning the scene back to a joke. Lars walks over and picks up the book, looking closely at the cover.

"Why does that guy have a sword?" he asks, quirking a brow at me. I laugh and shrug, then snatch the book back out of his hands.

"All these books have to have the Fabio type. Long hair,

muscles, a long thick sword," I muse, barely keeping my grin from my lips.

"Seems like a pretty thin sword to me," Lars says with a shrug. He turns his attention from the book in my hands to me. "I see what you're doing. Staring at that crappy book like it's your lifeline to getting out of this. You promised me a night of fun. It's time to deliver, Cal."

I frown at him, since I've never liked being called 'Cal.' It makes me sound like a small boy or a trucker with a hard-on for lot lizards. "Buuuut I don't want to have fun," I groan, setting the book on the table. "I want to get into my pajamas and lounge around. And I have to feed my goats."

"You don't have goats." Lars looks at me with suspicion.

"I could have goats," I reply with a sniff.

"You are coming out with me and that is final. You never do anything. You have no friends," he puts his hand up when I begin to argue, "other than me. Customers don't count."

I frown and cross my arms across my chest. "One hour."

"Six." He counters.

"Six? Gods, Lars, I have to open the shop in the morning!" I growl, stomping my foot like a petulant child.

"We'll have so much fun, you'll still be running on a high in the morning," Lars argues, and I know he's already won. I'll be going out because he's right. I don't have any friends.

"You're going to get me literally high, aren't you?" I ask him warily.

"Oh, don't be so uptight. Tonight will be a blast," he says with a smile, and I know that I'll live to regret this.

Chapter 2

Calluna

After an hour, I'm ready for my impending doom. I've squeezed my thick ass into the only 'night out' dress I have, and it hasn't been worn in about ten years. I stopped the party phase around twenty-four when I opened Beastie Besties, and now at thirty-four, I feel far too old to be at a nightclub.

The bouncer lets us in quickly, and I notice Lars eyeing him like a piece of meat. "Is he a possibility?" I ask, eyeing the muscular bouncer myself. His thick, corded muscles seem to be bursting out of his tight black t-shirt. Dark black sunglasses cover his eyes and draw my attention to a small silver nose ring, his thin lips framed by a black beard.

"For me, possibly. For you, possibly?" Lars replies, finally returning his attention to the scene in front of him. I look around the dark room that's lit only by spotlights and what looks to be an old disco ball. Ahhh, Vee. How you haven't changed.

I whisper yell to Lars over the music, squeezing closely

to him to avoid getting tangled in the crowd. "That doesn't sound very promising."

Lars shrugs. "Reggie is a confusing guy. I can't get a good read on him, but there's a strong possibility he swings both ways and I'm not a fan of sharing."

"Ahhh," I say with a nod. I look at my friend and wonder about him. He's also in his thirties, and it's probably time for him to drop the bar scene and settle down. Yes, yes. Kettle, pot, black. All that mumbo-jumbo, but at least I'm not still bar-hopping. I own a respectable business, and I'm responsible...for a lot of cats, but we'll just keep the last part to ourselves.

"Tonight's mission is to get you laid. I get laid every night." Lars smirks as the words leave his lips. I'm sure they're true, but that doesn't make them any less gross. I can only imagine the type of men he meets at Vee. Men that like bears. Not even the gay sort of metaphor, although kinda. He's a big gay guy, which makes him a bear in the stereotypical sense, but also, he's an actual bear shifter.

"I can do just fine on my own," I growl, joining him in looking over the club. Nada. Blood drunk vampires in their perpetual early twenties. Drunk shifters in their mid-twenties. Everyone is gyrating all over each other. Ugh, I'm sweating just looking at them.

I turn around and look away from the dance floor and over to the bar. There we have some more drunk shifters of different varieties, but all mostly old. Not my type of old either, but the sixty and up crowd. The type that lives in the bars. Then, I spot the bartender and sigh in relief.

"Rose!" I yell, weaving through the crowd to get to the bar. "How is Pumpkin?" I ask, feeling more at home talking about animals. I can deal with animal talk, not all the gyrating behind me.

Calluna

Rose smiles brightly, flashing a bit of fang in the bright light. "Hey, Calluna! I don't see you here often. Pumpkin is great! He's upstairs with Sam, sleeping I'm sure. I've been meaning to bring them both for a visit."

Rose and her mates own this bar, Vee, named as a play on vampire. Since they're all vampires, the name is kind of punny. A month ago, they brought in their cat that had recently been turned into a vampire. The most bizarre thing I'd seen, and I've seen some really bizarre shit. Like the wiener dog, Frank, that won't stop shitting glitter everywhere. Not as fun as it sounds. Oh, and Bingo the lizard that constantly escapes and brings random animals home with him. Since his current home is my pet store, he has turned into quite the handful.

I smile back at Rose, completely understanding why she has not been to the store lately. Her men, very sexy ones at that, do almost everything for her. They're the coddling type, and I think Rose doesn't mind the coddling much. "It's all good. I can get some more food made for him, how is his blood intake?"

"Are you fucking serious right now?" Lars rumbles as he comes up to the bar beside me. "I'll take a beer, Rose."

Rose nods and begins getting the beer. "What about you, Calluna?" she asks.

"Oh fuck, I don't know. Vodka and something?" I reply, completely clueless. "I'm sorry I don't drink or do anything really other than pet store stuff, but this asshole forced me out of reclusion."

Rose laughs and begins mixing me up a drink, then passes it to me. I take a sip and find it super delicious. I mouth 'thank you' to her and try to relax more. I close my eyes and listen to the music.

"Did you want to go upstairs? See Pumpkin? I'm sure

he'd love it. Logan can handle the bar for a bit," Rose asks with a smile, like she can tell I'm living in my own personal nightmare right now.

"Yes please," I moan, following her down the bar.

"Fine, but you better come back," Lars growls, pointing at me accusingly. He knows that I'm likely to ditch him, and he's right. This is just not my scene.

"You aren't coming with?" I ask, feeling bad for ditching my friend, even if it is to cuddle some cats.

"Nope. Never been a fan of pussy," Lars jokes before he weaves back through the crowd and begins grinding his dick against some man's ass. Well then. I turn to Rose and see her smiling at me near the door that heads into the back and what I'm assuming is the stairs to their loft.

Chapter 3

Calluna

When I get into the loft, I find one of Rose's mates, Sebastian, walking around in only a towel, and my mouth drops open. "Sorry, Seb. I brought up company. You remember Calluna?" Rose says nonchalantly, like I can't see the outline of her mate's cock through his towel.

Sebastian smiles at me, giving me a small wave. "Yup. Hi, Calluna. Sorry about this."

I smile back uncomfortably. "Oh, no problem at all. Sorry to barge in."

Rose frowns at me. "You aren't barging, I invited you."

"Oh great, the cat lady. Don't have any more furry fuckers with you this time, do you?" Finn asks, feigning annoyance. I know by the way he looks at Rose that if she wanted one hundred cats, he would comply. Might not like it, but he would comply.

"Actually, it's ferrets this time. Watch out for Klaus. Super sweet, but he has a horrible rash. Just put the ointment on every two hours," I explain, barely suppressing a smile.

"You'll love Klaus, babe. He looks just like you!" Rose teases, causing Finn's mouth to drop open like he just saw a half-naked Sebastian, cock outline and all.

"But. What? I don't—" He groans as if in pain. "Rosalie. Fuck. Where is he?" His eyes scan the room nervously.

Rose and I both crack up, and he sighs in relief. "There's no rashy ferret, is there?"

"Klaus is very real, I just haven't brought him," I say seriously. "No, I'm here to see this beautiful boy!" I squeal as Pumpkin sways into the room. I sit in the first chair I see and allow the chunky bundle of orange fur to leap into my lap and give me cuddles. "How is my favorite vampkitty?" I ask, kissing his soft cheeks.

"Fat. Lazy. Fucking his little cat broad all over the apartment. Living his best life," Finn says in irritation. He frowns at the love I give Pumpkin, and then he turns to Rose. "You don't really want to get a ferret, do you? Pumpkin would eat him."

Rose laughs, shaking her head. "No, no ferrets for me. You're probably right. Pumpkin would want to snack on him. I wouldn't say no to another cat though," she replies cheerfully.

His face drops a small bit before he's interrupted by a knock at the door. "Well, who the bloody hell is that? The party is downstairs!" he yells at the door just before opening it. The man that stands on the other side of the door is drop-dead gorgeous. Light brown skin accentuates all the black tattoos rippling against his muscles. I trail my eyes down his muscular body slowly, feeling my mouth water at the sight as I imagine all the dirty things I'd love to do to him. I finally get to his face and find myself continually impressed. A light scruff of black hair shades his chin, connecting to a buzz cut that is just as dark. His eyes have to be the lightest shade of brown I've ever seen and seem to have gold flecks in them.

"Calluna, this is Landyn. He works security for Vee. Landyn, this is Calluna. She owns the pet store, Beastie Besties, in town," Rose says brightly, introducing me to the delicious man in front of me that I recognize as the griffin shifter bouncer for the club. I remember the stories I heard from Lars about the man's trouble with the sphinx shifter that now resides at the prison in town.

Finn looks at her questioningly. "I'm sure they've met each other." He groans as her elbow jabs into his side.

"Nice to meet you," Landyn says softly, his eyes blazing with heat as he stares into mine.

"Hi," I reply, captivated by his gaze.

"This is fucking weird," Finn says quietly to Rose, causing her to jab him again and me to laugh. Finn's inability to catch on to the fact that Landyn and I are totally vibing right now is pretty humorous. Landyn only grows hotter when his eyes crinkle slightly as a smile graces his lips.

"Well, I need to go back to the bar, Logan is probably drowning in it. Come on, Finn," Rose says, grabbing him by the arm. Finn stares at us for a second longer as he follows Rose out. When Landyn and I are left alone in an apartment that isn't ours, it becomes awkward.

"I assume you came up here for a reason?" I ask awkwardly, trying to tame the fire that is burning at my core. This man is pure sex, and I can't help but imagine his strong hands grabbing my hips as he slams into me.

"I did," he replies, giving away nothing. I nod, pressing my lips together, unsure where to go from here.

Landyn just stares at me, his eyes penetrating my defenses, making me feel helpless.

"I don't do this often," I blurt out, immediately regretting it when I do.

A bright white smile crosses his lips. "Do what, exactly?"

"Go out. Come to Vee," I reply, shifting uncomfortably in my dress. "I'm normally in something much more comfortable."

My words give him the excuse to take in my body, and my core clenches as his eyes rove over me. I may be thick, but I know that I'm hot as fuck. I have the perfect amount of curves, and my thickness makes me capable of taking it rough. Boy, do I love it rough. I can tell he knows exactly where my mind is, based on the dilation of his pupils and the way his nostrils flare. *He can smell how wet I am.*

"I think I would like to see that," he growls, taking a step towards me.

My eyes widen slightly at his words, and I take into consideration that we aren't in our own home, that we're in Rose's and Sebastian is in the other room. I lick my lips unconsciously as I imagine allowing him to take me right here on their couch. "I would like to show you," I purr back.

Within a moment he is on me, a flash, and his hands have shot out, grabbing onto me. One hand takes my throat as his other grabs one of my breasts, and I relish in the roughness of it all. "Is this too much?" he asks, his voice cracking in its heaviness.

I stare into his eyes, baring my teeth. "More." My pussy arches into him, rubbing against his hardened cock straining in his jeans. All I want is for him to give it to me hard and rough. *I want to come*, my brain screams as I stare into his eyes.

"Your wish is my command," he says as his grip tightens

on my throat. "There are rooms downstairs. I don't think it would be wise for me to fuck on my bosses' couch." His deep voice and smirk only add to my slickness. I bite my lip, trying to refrain from purring like a cat in heat, and nod to him. He grabs onto my wrist and pulls me to the door and down the stairs, back into the madness.

Chapter 4

Calluna

The sudden darkness takes my eyes a bit to adjust to, since the only light is coming from the strobe lights streaking across the crowd. The atmosphere feels different than before, less terrifying and more electric. Mostly due to the strong hand that grips mine tightly as he pulls me through the crowd. When we get towards the back, he slips a key into a door that I'd never been in before, and I look at him questioningly.

"This room is just for employees," he says with a dark smile. As the door swings open, I take in the room before me. Dark red and black, the consistent theme of Vee, carries on in here. Black velvet curtains drop from the ceiling around a round bed covered in dark red silk. "It's cleaned often, if that's something you're worried about. The Whitakers have the Cleanly Den on retainer."

I nod, releasing my hand from his grip and walking towards the bed. My fingers drag across the soft silk, and I close my eyes as I imagine how it will feel against the rest of my body. I listen closely, hearing Landyn walk behind me, slowly coming closer. "Is this okay?" he asks again, and I feel a bit of warmness in my chest at his need to constantly make sure I am comfortable. I answer his question without words as I place my fingers on the strap of my dress and begin pulling it over my shoulder. His fingers cover mine, taking over the removal of my dress as his lips begin to caress my neck. When he has gotten both straps over my shoulders, he pulls the dress down farther, baring my heavy breasts pushed up in a black lace bra. His fingers continue their trail down, gently gliding against the skin on my stomach and then my hips, which reveals a pair of matching panties. When the dress has been pushed past my wide hips, it falls to the ground without a problem, and I squirm a bit as I feel Landyn spin me around in his arms so that he can see me from the front.

"You are unbelievably sexy," he growls, taking a step back to look me up and down. I stare him down unflinchingly, old enough to not feel self-conscious about my lack of a thigh gap or the fact that my stomach hangs over the waistband of my panties a bit. When his eyes finally get to my breasts, his tongue comes out and glides over his lips slowly. His large fingers slide across the top of my bra and pull down, causing my large breasts to bounce out. His eyes zero in on one of my nipples before dropping down to take one of the peaks in his mouth. My moans fill the room as I throw my head back, loving the feel of his lips against my sensitive nub and his rough beard dragging against the soft skin of my breasts. His hands fumble with the back of my bra, unhooking it and throwing it across the room before shoving me onto the bed. My long, dark brown hair fans around me as I bounce lightly on the bed. Before allowing him to cover me with his muscled form, I sit up, my fingers quickly pulling at his belt and popping open the button on his jeans. Pulling down his fly, I slip my fingers under the waistband of both his jeans and boxers, unwilling to undress him as slowly as he undressed me. I want him so much that there is sure to be a wet spot on the bed below me as I soak through my panties.

I yank down his pants and release his large cock, gasping at its thickness. By far the fattest cock I have ever seen in my life, it also has length and a slight upward curve that I know will rub me in all the right places. It's fucking beautiful. The kind of beautiful cock that you just want to sing songs about, although I know I must refrain. I slowly glance up and try to give him my sultriest stare, taking in his smug smile as he takes in my look of pure lust. I stare into his gaze as I reach my hand out and grab the base, squeezing gently and feeling it twitch in my grasp. When I lean forward and take it into my mouth, his groans match my own as I savor his smoky taste. My tongue swivels around the tip, licking up the pre-cum that has gathered there, then drags from the sensitive underside down to where my fingers still grasp the base. As my tongue drags back to the top of his crown, I feel the anticipation before I perform one of the sexual acts I'm most proud of. Getting your tonsils removed as an adult is fucking horrible. HORRIBLE. But I now have a handy little trick that seems to make the men wild—the lack of a gag reflex. I pull my lips around my teeth as I sink his monster cock into my mouth, feeling my lips stretch uncomfortably as he is much larger than I am used to. Never one to give up, I push on and relax my throat as I accept him deeper and deeper, knowing that I won't be able to take all of him. When the head of his cock hits the back of my throat, I feel his fingers sink into my hair gently.

"Fuuuuuck, Calluna." He groans out my name like a prayer. "How the fuck are you doing this?"

I moan as I slowly pull back before sliding back down. His fingers tighten on my hair as the vibrations do wonderful things to his cock. His fingers are never forceful as I allow him to fuck my mouth, almost soothingly. He growls loudly before pulling his cock from my hot, wet mouth, his grasp finding my throat again and pulling me up to his eye level.

His lips slam into my own, and our teeth clack together in the roughness of the kiss. His tongue delves into my mouth, and I get more turned on at the thought of him tasting himself on me. He breaks apart from me, his fingers tightening on my throat. "That was fucking amazing, seriously. But if I don't get inside you right now, I'm going to lose my fucking mind."

"No arguments here," I moan back, leaning back down onto the bed and pulling a soft pillow underneath my head. Landyn pulls his shirt off over his head and crawls onto the bed with me. He takes no time at all in getting my panties off and thrown to the floor with the rest of our clothes. I wait in anticipation, listening to the loud club music still beating in the background. He drags his tongue across my slit, and I squirm in surprise, caught off guard by his tongue instead of his cock, the scruff of hair on his chin doing wonderful things to my skin. His lips suck on my clit just before he slides up the rest of my body, caging me beneath him.

"I also needed to taste you," he says as his cock drags against my entrance. "I want to make you come in my mouth, but I can't wait any longer."

"Fuck me, please," I beg, arching my pussy into him as the head gets closer to my opening. I reach down and grab his cock, leveling it with my core and pushing up onto him, feeling the delightful stretch. He's much thicker than I'm used to, but I know that the pain mixed with my pleasure will be delicious. He strains as he pushes in, working to be slow and gentle as he stretches me to accommodate his thickness, but I want more. Need more. Curling my legs around him, I push him down into me with the heels of my feet digging into his ass.

"Luna," he gasps, the muscles in his neck and arms flexing. "I am holding on by a thread right now, and I don't want to hurt you," he growls, his brow furrowed.

"I'm not a dainty flower, Lan, now fucking shut up and fuck me hard," I snarl, getting closer to his face. He kisses me deeply as he shoves the rest of the way in. Shoves being the apt word, as I feel my body shatter beneath him as I take him in. My pussy clenches around him, feeling so close already, my eyes crossing as the pain and pleasure overtake me. My nails dig into his back, spurring him on as I thrust upwards. 'Fuck through the pain' has always been my motto, and it has never been more true than right now. Landyn groans as he begins to fuck me in earnest, one of his hands reaching down to thumb at my clit.

"You feel so fucking tight, so fucking wet for me," he rumbles as he slides in and out of me in the most delightful way, pulling every gasp from my lips. I quiver beneath him as the head of his cock drags against the sensitive spot inside me and his thumb continues to circle my clit.

"I'm close," I moan, arching up to put more pressure on my clit.

"Then come for me, baby girl. Give it all to me." Landyn growls, then he captures my mouth as I scream out my release.

Chapter 5

Calluna

I wake up with my legs interlaced with Landyn's, the different brown shades of our skin complimenting each other somehow. My hand slowly drifts against the hardness of his chest as I take one last feel before I flee. My core clenches achingly as I remember fucking him last night, his thickness stretching me to the limit but still leaving me begging for more. As I found out last night, Landyn is willing to give more. The time waiting for his cock to bounce back was spent with his head between my legs as he sucked and flicked at my needy clit. I came until it hurt, and then he made me come more before slamming his monster cock back into me. We fucked in every position possible, and I know I'll be walking out of this place bowlegged like I'd been riding a horse all day. Well, riding a griffin.

The only thing we took from each other was pleasure, leaving words for never. We both knew what this was, and I know that he won't be pained to see me gone before he wakes. I slip from the covers, enjoying the last touch of his smooth skin under my palm. Walking out of Vee in the daytime, in my nightclub dress, is going to be embarrassing enough without having the awkward morning after talk where we pretend that what this is will ever be more than just a night of hot, animalistic sex.

After jamming my body back into the skintight dress of last night, I slip on my shoes and walk towards the door. I can't find my underwear, but I'm unwilling to spend a minute longer in this room and risk him waking up. The maids of the Cleanly Den will dispose of them, magically, I hope.

I unlock the door and walk into the giant empty room that stands as the dancefloor for Vee, my heels echoing as they tap on the hardwood floor. I look around warily, glad to see that the room is empty and I don't have to have an embarrassing conversation with Rose or any of her guys. I speed up my steps, the exit in sight, when I hear a deep voice behind me. "Hi, Calluna."

Fuck.

I turn around to see Reggie walk out of one of the office rooms behind the bar, smiling at me knowingly. "Nice night?" he asks, a laugh in his voice.

"Very nice, thank you," I reply shortly as I continue to back towards the door, more than ready to escape this shit.

"Good. Have a good day." Reggie laughs, turning around to head back into the room he had just vacated. I sigh in relief as I slam my hands into the door and walk out into the brightness of the morning.

The worst part about the 'walk of shame'—besides the name of course, since there is nothing shameful about fucking a stranger—is the walk home because it's bright as fuck out and everyone knows by the look of you what you've been up to. People are out peopling and you're hungover, and in my case, waddling slightly after having your pussy blasted to smithereens by a griffin's monster cock.

I avoid the eyes of everyone I pass, groaning when I see Buttercup looking up at me from the window of her bakery. Especially when I walk into the entrance of my building and see my neighbor checking her mail.

"Good morning, Calluna," Violet says, giving me a disapproving once-over. "I assume you didn't dress like a...like a..." She waves a hand vaguely, indicating my outfit.

"A tart?" I ask.

"I didn't say that!" Violet flushes.

"Well, I don't know. I feel like I'm a tart at all times during the day," I say sassily, quirking my brow at her in annoyance.

"Mmmmmm," she hums in agreement, and her eyes light up with mischief. "Your animals were very loud last night, dear. I don't think the landlord would appreciate it."

"Well, you couldn't get him to keep the elevator running so you don't have to ride magical dildos down the stairs, so I don't think he'll start giving a fuck about my pets anytime soon," I hiss back. I don't hate the woman, I really don't. I'm just not in the mood this morning, and she knows it. "By the way, you're talking like an old person again."

"Language, dear," she replies pointedly, ignoring my comment about how she's speaking to me. "Besides, you know I don't need dildo rides anymore."

"Oh I know, I've seen the men. My animals aren't the only loud ones," I reply, smiling when I see her face flush as she realizes how her statement came off.

She tries to shrug off the comment, like she isn't embarrassed, and turns the conversation back to me. "Why are you walking like that?"

"Monster griffin cock, Vi. Blasted my pussy up," I state with a wide smile.

"That's..." Violet's cheeks flush, but in a way that tells me she's thinking of a griffin cock of her own. Or in Violet's case, I'm guessing troll cock. And the way she quickly waves goodbye and rushes upstairs tells me she'll be having one very soon.

I shake my head with a smile of my own as I fumble with the keys to my apartment, then unlock the door and automatically put my foot in front of the crack as I open it to keep all my animals inside. It was quite a surprise when I learned that my elderly librarian neighbor was actually a woman in her early twenties in disguise. Shit in Silver Springs is always weird.

I jump when I get inside and find that it's more than just my animals waiting for me.

"Fuck, Lars! What the hell are you doing here?" I yell out, dropping my keys to the floor. Immediately Binx, my black and tan dachshund, is all over them, smelling them before licking my ankles. I bend down and rub behind his ears, giving him a quick smooch, then snatch my keys back up.

"Well, you disappeared last night, so I got a little worried," he replies, staring at me with a smile.

"Worried?" I ask, already stripping out of the dress as I walk to my bedroom. I'm unconcerned about him seeing me in just my bra, though I do freeze before pulling the dress off my waist when I remember I lost my panties.

"More irritated. I figured you snuck out after talking with Rose and that I'd find you here in your granny panties and a giant t-shirt watching Netflix. So I hurried up and found someone to blow me in the alley, then headed this way ready to bust your ass," he explains, and I roll my eyes because of course he found someone to blow him in the alley.

Without skipping a beat, he goes on. "But I get here, use the spare key you gave me—"

"For *emergencies*," I cut in.

"Right, right. I come into your home, and what do I find? No Calluna," he says with a wide smile. He stands suddenly, walks over to me, and leans in to look closely at my side.

I snap my hand out and push him back. "What the hell are you doing?" I ask in surprise, looking down at the place he's staring at to find bruises in the shape of fingers around my waist.

"What is this, Cal? Who is the mystery man?" Lars asks in glee, returning to sit on my couch.

"Nobody," I state firmly as I walk out of the room and into my bedroom. I quickly strip from the dress, slipping on a pair of comfy underwear and leggings. I trade my strapless bra for a comfier alternative and pull on a t-shirt, knowing I need to get my ass in gear so I can open up Beastie Besties. I take in a deep breath and smell coffee brewing. *Bless you, Lars.* Running into the bathroom, I throw my hair up in a messy bun on the top of my head and brush my teeth. The makeup I had on last night looks fine enough after using a q-tip to get rid of the smudges under my eyes, and I walk back into the living room to find Lars standing there with my coffee in a to-go cup and a smile on his face.

"Hungover?" he asks with a smile.

"No," I reply, grabbing the coffee and taking a big drink.

"Sore pussy?"

I eye him in annoyance, knowing how pleased with himself he is. "Yes," I growl, slipping my feet into some flip flops before walking out the door.

"You're welcome," he says with a wide grin as he follows me out the door. I can't help but roll my eyes as I smile back.

"Shut up. So who did you find to blow you in the alley?" I ask, mildly curious.

"Oh, nobody special." He shrugs. "On to the next one. But you, you need to spill. Who did you spend the night with?"

"Just someone that works at Vee," I reply stoically.

"I'm gonna need more than that," he says, before frowning in concentration. "Logan? Oakley?"

"No to both."

"Then who? Just tell me, Cal," he groans, and then takes a drink of his own coffee, looking at me with puppy dog eyes.

"Landyn," I say with a small quirk of my lips.

"Shut the fuck up!" Lars says with a loud guffaw. "I knew you had a thing for broken animals, but not broken men."

Chapter 6

Landyn

My body is rigid when I wake up and not in a good way. Sweat drenches my skin, and I feel the silken bedspread sticking to me uncomfortably. I blink repeatedly to try to erase the images of my nightmares from my mind, but it never works. Feeling my heart beat out of control as adrenaline rushes through me, I startle when I hear a knock at the door.

"You okay in there, Lan?" asks my supervisor and closest friend through the wood of the door. *Lan.* I focus on the words, remembering her moaning them last night. The scratches on my back and shoulders burn slightly, but in a good way—a nice burning memory of the night's events. When the door pushes open, I grab the blanket on the bed to cover my semi-hard cock from Reggie.

"I saw Calluna leaving this morning," Reggie tells me with a smile. "She seemed to be in a hurry to get out of here and didn't seem happy to see me."

"No, I don't suppose she was. I'm sure you made things uncomfortable," I say with a shake of my head.

Reg just shrugs and walks further into the room, grabbing my jeans from the floor and tossing them to me. "She's good for you. I'm glad to see you getting back out there."

I frown at him as I pull the jeans onto my body. "She's nothing," I growl, knowing the words aren't true as they leave my lips. "And I'm not getting back out there. Last night was a mistake."

Reg shakes his head at me, a look of disappointment crossing his features. A look I am getting all too used to. "Landyn, you gotta get over this shit. You are so far in your fucking head that you aren't the same person anymore. That shit with Shani is in the past, and I know you won't fucking believe me, but it wasn't your fault."

My shoulders immediately tense, and I feel my hands close into fists. *Shani.* Just the sound of that bitch's name makes me want to punch something. Shani and her brother Ausar moved to town and took up jobs at the local police station. We don't have a huge amount of supernatural law enforcement in Silver Springs, so their appearance was a surprise to many. Little did we know that Shani was obsessed with vampires and not in a good way. Hellbent on avenging her ancestors, who she believes were made almost extinct due to vampires, she began targeting vampires and their businesses in town. As I'm a griffin shifter and not a vampire, it shouldn't have involved me, but her obsession grew to taking down the Whitakers and Vee, my employers. As one of the heads of security, it wasn't surprising that her path crossed with mine, even though we didn't know it was her that was targeting the bar at the time.

A little-known fact about sphinx shifters is they have the power to manipulate the minds of others, including other supernatural beings. One night on my rounds, she got me alone, and then I was hers to direct. Her slave. Although I could sense what was happening to me, I could do nothing to stop it. It was like I was trapped in my own body while someone else had the controls. The things she made me do —I grit my teeth, forcing the images out of my head.

"I'm fine," I growl out, pushing myself up off the bed. I find my t-shirt on the floor by the door, haphazardly thrown across the room last night, then grab it and pull it over my head. I need to go home, shower, and change.

"I want you to take the night off," Reggie says pointedly, putting his muscled arm between me and the door. "We have Oakley and a few others working tonight. Take the night, clear your head."

"I thought that's what last night was?" I ask sarcastically with a quirk of my brow. "I fucked a customer last night while I was on the clock. Aren't you supposed to be ripping into my ass instead of giving me the night off?"

Reggie smiles at me, shaking his head. "Consider me your fairy fucking godmother. Now go home and get some sleep. Maybe call Calluna."

I glare at him until he moves his arm, but he chuckles because he knows I'll listen to him. Or at least, he thinks I will. I'll take the night off and get some sleep, but I will not be calling Calluna. The last thing I need to do is drag a woman into the insanity that is my life.

I walk through Vee, thankful that the Whitakers are all sleeping so I don't have to suffer through any uncomfortable confrontations. The guys would be fine, but Rose sees too much and would definitely interrogate me about last night. I walk around the corner to find my SUV sitting where I left it last night, the bright sun reflecting off the black paint. I get inside and take a deep breath, clutching the steering wheel too tightly, the images of all the Shani shit flashing through my head like I'm some kind of fucking PTSD victim.

Heh, I guess I am.

I drive through town, trying to get to my house as soon as possible. I can tell that I'm going to break down, and I want to be in my home when it happens. If I can just get there, then I can take all this fucking energy out on my punching bag or set a small fire. Fucking cathartic shit.

I drive down the same road I do every single day, just in time to see the one thing I didn't want to—Calluna and her male coworker walking down the street together towards her pet store. She has stripped from last night's clothes and is now wearing yoga pants and a loose-fitting t-shirt, still somehow looking just as sinfully beautiful as when she was in that black dress. Her long, dark brown hair is thrown up in a messy bun on top of her head, and I see her face flush as our eyes connect and her chest moves as if she's letting out a loud gasp. *Fuck.* I keep driving, ignoring what she does to my senses, and keep my eyes on the road. Five more minutes. Five more fucking minutes, and I'm there.

Five more fucking minutes.

Chapter 7

Calluna

Lars and I stand in the same spot we were in when Landyn drove by, leaving me feeling like a fucking idiot. *What the fuck?*

"Whew. That man makes my cock hard," Lars says, breaking the silence.

"What the fuck, Lars?" I bark out, shocked, then laugh because I can't hold it back. "There is something seriously wrong with you."

"What? You see how sexy he is! Plus that fucking look he gave you." He shivers as if overcome by whatever look he thinks he saw. There was no look. I'm sure I had a 'deer in headlights' look, which is super sexy. *Not.*

"Let's just go," I groan, walking ahead.

"Wanna know what makes him that much sexier?" Lars asks as he jogs a bit to catch up with me.

"Nope. Don't wanna know," I reply curtly.

Lars goes on like he didn't hear me. "Just watching you walk. Holy fuck, that man must be packing something magical to make you walk like you have a stick shoved up your ass." He quickly dodges my sad attempt to punch him, guffawing in laughter. "I suppose in your case, it'd be more like a log shoved up your cunt."

I make a loud disapproving noise before spitting out, "You're fucking crass. I hate that word."

"Oh, I do apologize, Ms. Daisy. I do declare that the young fellow surely must have boned you with quite an enormous cock. Toodle pip!" He stops and bows low to me like a character out of a Jane fucking Austen novel.

"I hate you."

"No, you don't," he admonishes, pulling me into his side. "You love me more than anyone else."

I shake my head, trying my hardest to push myself out of his grasp. Suddenly, my eyes fall on a store I've never seen before, and I stop in my tracks. We're still two blocks away from Beastie Besties, so Lars looks at me strangely until his gaze moves to where mine is focused.

"Black Moon Magick," Lars says, reading the sign hanging above the door.

"Do you feel that?" I ask as I sense negative energy coming off the store in waves.

Lars seems to shiver, then nods his head. "Yes, let's go, Calluna." He grabs my hand and starts to pull me in the direction toward my shop, but I don't budge.

"I want to go in," I whisper, my eyes glued to the windows that are covered in blue curtains as dark as the night sky.

"What the fuck? Nope. I didn't learn a lot from my family, but I learned enough to know that something with that kind of energy is as good as a giant fucking sign screaming 'get the fuck out,'" Lars says, pulling me with more strength and causing me to stumble a bit.

I look at him pointedly, trying to keep my feet planted. "What if this place is connected to whoever is cursing the animals?" I hiss out, side-eyeing the store.

Lars' lips form a frown, and his whole body goes rigid before he relents, looking at me angrily. "Five fucking minutes. We go in, look around, then get the fuck out."

"Deal," I say with a slight smile, pleased to have gotten my way. Fear floods my chest, but I push it down as I take a step towards the door and pull on the handle.

The typical *ding* sounds above us as the door opens, alerting the store owner to our presence. A tall man with olive skin and high cheekbones turns to face us. Bright white hair drapes over his shoulder, partially tied back at the top in half a ponytail and revealing large pointed ears. A high elf.

"Hello there," says the man in a stilted voice, eyeing us carefully. "I am Falcar, welcome to my store."

I smile at him weakly, my eyes scanning the room—for what, I don't know. A sign that says, 'I curse animals'? "I'm Calluna."

"Ahhh." He sighs the word. "You own the delightful little pet store down the road. Beastly Beasties?"

"Beastie Besties, but yes, that's me. Are you new to town? I've never seen you before," I question him, continuing to walk around and look at the items he's selling.

"Yes," he says, stepping nearer to me. His eyes are watching me closely. "Silver Springs is quite the *quaint* little town. More openly supernatural than most towns in the area. I figured it would be a good place to set up shop."

"Have you had a lot of business?" I ask, flinching a bit at my rudeness.

"Not so far, no. You are the first." He pauses, walking over to me and picking up the black stone necklace I was looking at. "This is a protection amulet. It repels any kind of unwanted magical residue from attaching to you, best used when working more...sinister magic."

My lips form a frown, and I nod in acknowledgment. "Most people aren't so open about practicing dark magic. Do you not fear persecution from the people of the town?"

He gives a long and almost condescending laugh. "You walked in, did you not? Everyone is curious about the dark side of magic, even if they are unwilling to admit it. It's addictive in its nature. It is exotic and seductive. Before you know it, you're just practicing magic with no regard to the *light* or *dark* qualities."

He says the words as if he truly believes they're true. As if he could convert the town of Silver Springs to openly practicing dark magic. No one would be accepting of that. I shake my head unconsciously, and he laughs again.

"You do not believe me?" he asks, drawing my gaze to his. "You think that those around you would not accept your darker nature, *changeling*?"

My teeth grind together, and I eye him warily. Lars grabs my arm for the second time today and begins pulling me out of the store. "Let's go, Calluna," he says quietly, not looking back as he drags me out.

"I'll be seeing you, Calluna," Falcar says, enunciating each syllable of my name.

Lars and I walk in silence to the pet store, and I dread each step we take, knowing that once we get there, he'll have questions. My best friend of seven years never knew that I was a changeling. *A dark elf*. I should have hightailed it out of that store once I saw that the owner was an elf. I shouldn't have ever taken Lars in there. I should've come back by myself.

When we get to the front door of my store, I fumble with

the keys as I unlock the door. We get inside, and immediately, I'm greeted by Lina, the tortoiseshell cat that lives here full time. I've tried to take her home multiple times, but she hates it and drags her butt the whole way.

"Hi, Lina," I croon, rubbing behind her ears as she purrs loudly.

"We aren't going back there. That guy was a fucking freakshow," Lars growls out.

"Yeah, he was very strange," I agree, avoiding his eye.

"What did he mean about your darker nature?" he asks as he sits in one of the chairs in the room.

"Not sure," I reply, moving to busy myself with getting the shop ready to open up. I walk around checking food and water bowls, saying hi to all the animals that appear excited to see me. Klaus runs up to Lars and jumps on his lap, bringing my attention back to him.

"Hi, Klaus!" Lars exclaims, petting the adorable ferret. I grab the ointment from behind the counter and toss it to him. He catches the ointment with a grimace but immediately begins unscrewing the cap.

"How much longer do you think we'll be lathering up this little guy?" he asks, globbing some of the medication onto Klaus, who sits there looking like he is loving every minute of it.

"Until he gets adopted, but I'm not sure how long it will be until the rash goes away," I say, my mouth twisting in worry. I walk over to the door and flip the 'closed' sign to 'open,' then get back to my normal chores, hoping with all my might that Lars doesn't pursue questioning me on any darkness the dark mage saw in me.

Chapter 8

Rhett

My fingers dig deeper into Damian's sculpted abdomen as I slam into him harder and harder, his grunts of pleasure spurring me on. I feel the roar of pleasure filling my own abdomen as my body prepares to come, and I race to that finish line.

"I'm close," I growl, my other hand reaching down lower to grasp his throbbing cock.

"Fuuuuck, Rhett," Damian moans as I begin pumping him faster, wanting him to finish with me. By the way he pulses in my fist, I know that my wish is about to come true. "Oh fuck, Rhett, I'm coming!" he yells in ecstasy, just as I bottom out one last time, my cum shooting into his ass. I roar my release and free his cock from my grasp, collapsing on top of his back. We're both covered in sweat, and I have the urge to drag my tongue against his smooth, salty skin.

When I pull my softened cock out of him and drop to the bed beside him, he rolls over and places a hand on my chest. "Fuck, that was good," I groan out, my breath still coming out in pants.

"It's always fucking good," Damian replies with a cocky smile. "Next time, I'm taking you," he growls, and my cock has the nerve to twitch. *Fuck, this man is insatiable.*

"I'm always game for that," I reply, looking at him and still feeling strong feelings of lust. It's been a couple of years, but fuck, everything about Damian continues to surprise the shit out of me. I've never had a relationship with a man, just the standard one-night stand, but this man kept me coming back. Coming and coming.

I've lived my life under ridicule, being a fennec fox shifter. Fox shifters are mostly hated in the supernatural community for being sneaky, untrustworthy, and overall ruthless. Add in the fact that I'm a fennec fox? Well, I'm seen as a tiny, deceitful bitch. I moved away from my family's community at twenty-one when I realized that I had no interest in settling down with a vixen fennec and continuing to live that backwoods way of life—literally one with the forest, born to work in the mine, and shoot a litter of kits out with my mate. *No thank you.* Besides, their backwoods ways of thinking also didn't look too kindly on me being bisexual. I've always found myself attracted to a person versus a singular gender. Men, women, I'll take 'em both.

That's what brought me to Silver Springs. A town filled with supernaturals had to be more accepting than where I was from, and I was mostly right. Sure, there are baddies here, just like everywhere else. Beefed up fuckers that think it's wrong for a man to fuck a man or a woman to fuck a woman, but for the most part, everyone is very accepting. Especially since many of the supernaturals in these parts seem to live a polyamorous lifestyle, something I've been drawn to since I first saw it in action. A woman walking down the street surrounded by men that were head over heels in love with her. *Living as a family.* Dammit, I want that.

"Do you know what I feel like?" Damian asks, interrupting my thoughts.

"Baby, I'm gonna need a minute," I moan, then lean over and press his soft lips to mine.

"Not that...yet," he growls back at me, kissing me back passionately. "Let's go for a run. It's been a while."

I nod, not removing my fingers from his hair and biting his lower lip gently. Okay, maybe I'm just as insatiable as he is. But fuck, this man is sexy as hell.

"Let's go," he says, pulling himself from my grasp and getting off the bed. I take a moment to take in the view of his tight ass as he stands up and bends over to grab his jeans from the floor. He pulls them onto his body, commando. *Fucking hell.*

I pull myself off the bed and grab some pants for myself, skipping the shirt as it's not needed for a run in the woods and it's easier to just magic a pair of pants in and out of existence versus a whole damn outfit. I look over to see that Damian is forgoing a shirt too.

"You are so fucking sexy," he says to me, stealing the words straight out of my head.

"You too, babe," I growl back, my voice still thick with lust. "Let's go."

When we get to the edge of the woods, just a short walk from my home, Damian shifts. His form drops to the ground, flashing a bit before I see the small animal that lives inside him.

"Well, hello there, little guy," I croon, reaching out to pet the small meerkat's head. He makes a barking noise at me, biting at my hand. "Don't be so uptight. You're small," I reply with a laugh, stretching my neck to the side before I let my body shift. I drop down to about the size of Damian, my fennec fox rubbing against his meerkat. He makes that barking noise again, and I reply with my own chirping sound.

Then we're off, sprinting through the darkness of the forest faster than most of the animals around us. Our little legs easily dodge through the underbrush, running as if we were prey. Which we are. There are quite a few species of shifters that would enjoy chasing us, just to be assholes. That is just one of the joys that Damian and I have to live with, something that has bonded us together.

The loud sound of a pained screech causes us both to freeze in place, our heads snapping in the direction of the noise. We slowly creep towards where the sound came from, our bodies close to the ground and ready to move in the other direction if needed. We have no fear of the natural wildlife around here, although many coyotes would love to catch us, but as soon as we shift back to our human forms, they run away in fear.

As we approach the edge of some brush, there is a clearing in front of us with a stone in the middle. A man in all black stands before a small animal, his figure somehow shrouded in an equally black colored smoke. He mumbles words that I don't understand as his hand hovers above the animal, once again pulling another yowl from its throat. I take a small step forward, leaning in to try to see what the animal is, when I see its tail flip agitatedly. *It's a fucking dog.* Without thinking, I lunge, but a twig snaps beneath my small paws as I leap into the air. The man turns to face me, a growl leaving his lips, his face shrouded in the dark smoke. He spits out more of the foreign words before swinging his hand at me, causing a plume of the same smoke to slam into me. More of the strange words leave his lips, then everything in my vision turns black.

Chapter 9

Calluna

I look over at the clock and see that it's already almost ten o'clock at night. I sent Lars home a while ago when I realized that today was going to be a slow one. I had planned to read that book, but instead, got distracted by my phone. Stupid Screech. Ever since the supernatural version of Facebook popped up, I got sucked in, like most of the town it seems. I mostly scroll through to see if there's anything strange going on with the pets in town. I don't know what I'm expecting to see. It's not like the asshole cursing animals is going to just throw up a status update.

Cursing animals for fun lolz.

I shake my head to myself as I scroll through the newsfeed. Seeing that Jewels Cafe has a coupon for five percent off, I use the clip function to save it, then do the same when I see Highway to Spells also has a deal going on. Most of my antidotes, including Klaus' rash cream, are made with ingredients I get there.

My phone nearly drops from my hand as my front door slams open. I leap to my feet, adrenaline rushing through me as I stare at the man bursting into my shop. His skin is a dark tan color, and he's showing off more of it than I'm used to seeing in a public place. He stands in the doorway, shirtless, holding a small fennec fox and a dog. I immediately rush to him, looking over the animals closely.

"What happened?" I ask, observing the fox that seems to be unconscious and has black tendrils of smoke leaking from its small mouth.

"He's a shifter," the man gasps, shoving the fox into my arms. "We were running and came upon a man torturing this dog. He turned and attacked us before vanishing into thin air."

I nod my head, trying to examine the fox for wounds, then moving on to the dog. Gashes are cut into the dog's skin, leaking the same black smoke. I pull up its eyelids to find them cloudy and skin failing to snap back as it should. "The dog is dead," I say quietly, my heart wrenching in pain.

This is completely different from what I've seen so far in the cursed animals brought into my shop, and it causes fear to rush through me. "Can you rouse the fox to shift back?" I ask, knowing it will be easier to help a man in human form versus shifted form.

The man looks at me with concern, his fingers grazing against the fox's fur. "I've tried, but he won't wake up!" Fear radiates off him in waves, and I touch him gently on the arm, hoping to calm him. He gives me a weak smile before turning back to the fox.

"Give me your number and leave him with me. I'll do my best and call you in the morning," I tell him, stiffening when I see his head immediately begin to shake in defiance.

"I will not leave him!" the man growls, looking at me with anger and suspicion.

I eye him warily, as I'm scared to perform any kind of magic in front of the stranger. Especially dark magic. His eyes plead with me, pulling at my heartstrings, and I sigh loudly before giving him my nod of acceptance. Maybe he won't recognize what I'm doing. Maybe he won't realize.

I rush over to the small cabinet in the back where I store all my dark items, pulling keys from my pocket to unlock the door. The items inside range from typical smudge sticks and crystals to items of the more sinister variety. I grab a bottle of neem oil, coarse sea salt, anise, and a darker vial containing blood. *My blood.* I rush over to the table where the man stands next to the two animals, his focus now solely on the fox.

"What is your name?" I bite out, looking at him seriously and considering whether he is trustworthy.

"Damian. My name is Damian," the man gasps out, his voice sounding thick.

"Lock the doors, Damian," I demand. "Close the curtains and turn off the lights."

Without a word, he immediately begins following my directions, rushing through the motions. After he steps away, I grab a knife and cut a small chunk of hair from the fox and put it into a small bowl, pouring the neem oil over it. I begin chanting the words that have become all too familiar to me lately, my hand hovering over the bowl. A spark releases from my hand, igniting the hair and oil with a loud pop. Damian's attention snaps back to us, and he moves over to stand near me. I mix the anise with my blood, adding the salt to the mixture and holding my hand above. The mixture calls to me, its whispered words telling me what it is missing—more blood.

"Give me your hand," I snap, reaching for Damian's hand that he hesitantly moves toward me. With one swift motion, I slice his hand with my knife, squeezing it into a fist and holding it above the mixture, watching as his blood drips into the bowl.

"What the fuck—" Damian spits out, but I push his hand away, muttering more words over the bowl before pouring it over the burning neem oil. When the liquids meet one another, they begin to bubble and pop loudly, turning into a thicker liquid that's more like syrup.

"Hold him," I growl as I grab the bowl. Damian looks at me questioningly, but does what I say and holds on to the tiny fox. I pry the fox's jaws open and pour the bubbling liquid into his mouth. Seconds pass where nothing happens, then it screeches. Barks and yips mix to create a gut-wrenching noise that appears to destroy Damian. He holds the fox closely to his chest, looking at me angrily.

"What the fuck did you do?" he yells, anger marring his otherwise handsome face. "What is wrong with him?" I cringe as he bellows the question before he moves on to chanting the fox's name. "Rhett. Rhett. Please wake up. Rhett."

One last screech sounds loudly and rattles in my chest, just as the small animal coughs and retches, allowing the black smoke to billow out of his mouth. Blood sprays from its mouth with the smoke, and I relish in the knowledge that it is mine and Damian's being pushed out with the vile smoke.

"Rhett. What the fuck, man?" Damian sobs, holding the fox closely to his chest. The fox coughs one last time, deep and hard, forcing the last of the smoke out, and then within seconds, he shifts. Damian no longer clutches a tiny fennec fox to his chest, but instead, a completely naked male with blond-streaked hair and sun-tanned skin. "Rhett," he croons, the words no doubt coming from a lover as they caress their intended recipient.

I make to back away, to leave Damian with Rhett and to give the men their moment. I also need to dispose of the poor dog that I was unable to save, but Damian stops me with a single word.

"Thanks," he rasps, his fingers sliding through Rhett's hair and gently grazing the skin on his face.

"Anytime," I reply, my voice cracking on the words. "I'll give you a moment..." I lift the dog and carry it toward the back of my shop. My fingers swipe at tears as they streak from my eyes, several emotions attacking me at once. Witnessing the love between the two men was heart-wrenching, especially seeing Damian as he believed that Rhett was lost. Losing the dog, even though it was mostly gone before they even arrived. Then the knowledge that I just performed dark magic in front of a stranger. Fed another stranger my blood along with that of Damian's. Fuck. I am so screwed.

Chapter 10

Calluna

When I walk back into the main room of my store, I see that Damian has pulled Rhett onto one of the couches I keep along the wall, still holding him to his chest. I smile slightly at the sight, walking over to the table Rhett and the dog just vacated to clean up the mess I'd left. I wipe away the remains of blood and other...*debris* left over from removing the curse from Rhett. I've performed the ritual several times, but never on a shifter. All of the cursed animals I've seen thus far have been true animals, mostly animals belonging to those of magical backgrounds or animals that have the potential to become familiars. This...well, this is completely unprecedented. That a mage, whether dark or not, would attack a shifter is risky. Riskier than I have seen of this monster so far.

"What are you?" Damian asks, and I turn to him to see that he's staring at me.

"I am a pet store owner," I reply tersely, going back to my task at hand.

"Bullshit," Damian growls. I hear his hand rubbing against Rhett's back, and it softens my frown a bit.

"Why did you bring him here? Why not take him to a hospital?" I question, turning to face him again.

Damian shrugs. "Because I've heard of what you can do. That you specialize in cursed animals."

I sigh loudly, grabbing the rest of my items and shoving them back into the cabinet and locking the door. "Is that what I'm known for?"

"It's well-known that you sell cursed animals, although they're always much less cursed than when they were brought to you. You were the only person I could think of," Damian explains, still looking at me suspiciously. "What you did to him—"

"I'd appreciate it if you kept that between us," I respond tersely.

He looks at me carefully, staying silent for what feels like an eternity. "Okay."

"Thank you. I'd suggest you stay out of that forest, as he will hold a mark. Not a physical one, but whatever attacked him may still be drawn to him," I explain, then pause. "What forest were you in?" I ask, hoping to gain more information on the monster doing this.

"Just on the northern edge of town. I believe some bears are living out there, as well as some other shifters. It's near Rhett's home, so we tend to run there a lot," he explains, his eyes drawn back to Rhett.

"Bears," I repeat. "I have a friend that lives out there. I'll see if he's ever seen anything unusual like this. In the meantime, you both can stay here tonight. I have a few air mattresses in the back. It comes in handy when I need to watch an animal all night. You're welcome to one of them."

"Thank you, for everything," Damian says before quietly whispering sweet nothings to Rhett.

I wake up when the room is drenched in so much sunlight that squeezing my eyes shut doesn't help to block the light out. I listen as heavy footsteps that I recognize well walk towards me, stopping at the edge of my makeshift bed.

"Good morning, Calluna," Lars says with laughter in his voice. "There is a naked man in the bed over there. Care to explain?"

"Mmmhmm," I moan, trying to open my eyes in the bright light.

"These guys last night and Landyn the night before? Damn, I've never been prouder!" His voice cracks mockingly, and I open my eyes enough to see him dramatically clutching his chest.

"If I'd fucked them, wouldn't we all be in a bed together?" I ask in annoyance.

Lars shrugs. "I dunno, you don't seem like the type that would be up for sharing a bed. I can see you taking a bed to yourself after you've been satisfied."

I make a *tsk* noise as I pull myself up from the bed, stretching and pulling my hair into a messy bun on the top of my head. I try to think of a reason to give Lars for the men being here, since I'm unwilling to tell him that I've been doing dark magic, let alone performing it on and in front of strangers.

"Our dog was cursed last night. He didn't make it," Damian says sleepily, pulling himself into a sitting position on the bed and looking over at Rhett to make sure the sleeping man is okay. I close my eyes and try to pull from his energy, finding it much easier now that he has ingested some of my blood. "My boyfriend was wounded in the process and shifted unconsciously, without his clothes it seems."

Lars' lips form a frown, and he nods, not unused to cursed animals being brought into the store, although their owners don't usually stay the night. "I have some clothes in the back." He eyes Rhett slowly...much too slowly for Damian's liking, causing the man to growl. "They'll be big on him, but they'll work." Lars walks to the back of the store to grab the sweatpants he keeps stored there.

'Thank you,' I mouth to him, not daring to say the words out loud as I know Lars would hear them.

Damian nods his head, then turns to wake up Rhett. "Rhett. Rhett, we need to go home," he says, shaking the man. Rhett startles awake and looks around the room warily.

"Where are we?" he asks, looking to Damian with no fear, only confusion. It's clear he feels safe with the other man.

"I'll explain everything when we get home," Damian whispers to him, and Rhett nods back. As Lars walks into the room, Rhett finally notices that he's stark naked on the bed. He grabs a blanket to cover up his cock, looking at Lars and me awkwardly. Lars throws Rhett the sweatpants, and we turn to allow him to put them on. I walk over to the checkout counter and grab one of my cards, flipping it over to write my cell number on the back. I hand the card to Damian as he and Rhett walk to the door to leave.

"Call me if you need anything or if anything changes," I say in a low tone.

Damian takes the card, nodding to me and shoving it in his back pocket. "Thank you, Calluna."

Chapter 11

Calluna

When they're gone and I can no longer see them walking down the street, I turn away from the front windows and walk back into the main area of the store. Lars looks at me curiously, a knowing smile on his lips.

"Very sexy men," he says, bending over to let the air out of the mattresses.

"Yes, I suppose they were," I reply, folding blankets and shoving them in the back room.

"Spent the night?" he goes on, drawing this out.

"Mmhmm."

"Calluna, what the fuck happened here?" he asks, finally cutting the bullshit.

"What Damian said. Their dog died," I reply as I sit down on the couch.

"I saw the dog, so that part checks out. But they stayed the night? This all seems very strange," Lars goes on, looking at me oddly. "Did you have a threesome last night?"

"What? No, of course not," I say dismissively. Although all the crazy shit aside, both men were very attractive. "Lars, I'm tired as hell, and my body aches something fierce. This is the second night I haven't slept for shit. Think you can handle the store today?"

"Of course, I will. Go home. You need a day off anyway," he says, motioning towards the door.

"Thank you," I tell him sincerely, then put my face in my hands. He walks over and lays his hands on my shoulders, rubbing them gently.

"I know how hard it is for you when you lose one. You can't save 'em all, Cal," he tells me in an attempt to make me feel better.

"But I should. This shit shouldn't be happening," I groan, rubbing my forehead. "Thank you, Lars. I really appreciate you. Call me if you need anything."

"Go. I won't need anything." He pushes me toward the door, grabbing my purse with the hand that isn't currently shoving me toward the door.

I walk home without any trouble, relishing the fact that none of my neighbors see me walking into my apartment in the morning after having been gone all night for the second time in a row. Two nights spent with very sexy men? Very unlike me. Granted, I didn't have sex the second night. Still, that's a new one.

I jump when Jake leaps into my arms, making me drop my purse. "Hi, baby boy," I coo at the small capuchin monkey as he rubs his face into mine. I kiss his cheek and he meows loudly in encouragement. I smile widely as he immediately jumps out of my arms and begins galloping through the apartment on all fours like a horse. I follow the small galloping monkey into my bedroom and watch as he jumps into my bed and points at the pillow and then at me accusingly. "I know, I know. Two nights in a row is a bit much, isn't it?" He nods at me in acknowledgment, as if he understands me.

When Jake came to me, he was in horrible shape. It was as if he were being forced into being another species, and he would flash and semi-shift into each animal. He was one of the first animals I found when this all started, and I tried my hardest to save him. I read articles and found books about dark magic, but I left it too late. Or maybe I just didn't perform the spells correctly, and now poor Jake is stuck in a non-stop cycle of species. He mostly just falls somewhere between horse and cat though, when he isn't being a monkey. Another unlucky creature that I was only able to partially remove the curse from. Stuck with a species disorder, Jake believes that he is several different animals, and I have yet to find a way to help him. Though, he fits in well in my land of misfit pets.

I lie down on my bed, staring at the ceiling and trying to focus on what has happened to me over the past few days. I can't help the ache in my chest at the thought of the dog Damian and Rhett found being tortured to death. The image of the Australian Shepherd mix lying on the table in my shop is burned into my memory, and I squeeze my eyes tightly closed to try to force the image out. I ignore the movement on the bed as Jake jumps off and goes into the other room. *A nap, that's what I need*, I think, settling into the bed on my side and pulling my blanket up under my chin and between my legs. The bed shifts again as Jake jumps back onto the bed, and I groan.

"On or off, make your decision," I say loudly, keeping my

eyes closed. Jake begins chirping, sounding like a mix of his monkey self and the sounds a cat makes when it sees a squirrel outside. I crack an eye open to glare at him when I see what's in his hands.

Love Blooms by C.C. Pine.

I look at the cover, shaking my head again at the ridiculousness of it all. "Where did you get that?" I scold gently, hating when he digs through my purse. He makes the chirping noise again, pushing the book towards me, and I grab it. "Why not?" I say out loud, speaking to no one in particular.

I skim through the pages, reading the dedication to the author's sweetheart, and I roll my eyes. I don't feel like a story right now, I need the business, like when you're a kid and you smack your Barbie and Ken dolls together. I need that, so I skim through to find some of the raunchier bits of the story. As I read, I find my eyes feeling heavier and heavier, until I feel the book hit my chest as I fall asleep.

Chapter 12

Landyn

My chest clenches as I feel a sudden pull, an irresistible pull out of my apartment, as if someone has connected a string to my chest, but I begin to feel unrelenting fear. *Shani*. Could she still have influence over me? I search frantically for my phone, finding it on my nightstand where I left it. I slide my finger across the touch screen and scroll through my messages, searching for my buddy Adam's name. He works at Silver Springs Penitentiary in the section Shani is kept in.

Landyn: Any news?

I text him, waiting on pins and needles for a reply. Within seconds, a text flashes on my screen as my phone vibrates in my hand.

Adam: No news. She was moved to a fortified cell to prevent her from trying to manipulate the guards. Are you okay?

Landyn: I'm good. Thanks, man.

I shove my phone into my pocket and let out a deep

breath I didn't realize I was holding. I flex my fingers, feeling awkward that I flipped out just now. Shani is in a cell, and she will be for a long time. There is no way she could be using any kind of magic from this distance anyway. The penitentiary is several miles outside of town, and not even she could perform anything from that distance.

I pull out my cell again and look at my calendar, seeing if I work tonight and feeling relief that I do. Anything to get me out of the house, even if it is forced interaction. I walk over to my dresser and grab a pair of jeans and pull them onto my body, thinking of the last time I was in Vee the night before last—spending the night with Calluna. I wince as I feel that tugging sensation again, shaking it off to horniness as I think about her thick waist and the way her big tits jiggled as I slammed into her.

Fuck. I sure do know how to scare them off, how to make myself completely closed off so that I spend the rest of my days alone. Is that what I truly want? To avoid ever feeling anything for anyone? To avoid giving anyone any kind of power over me, so that I never feel like I did when Shani took over my mind again? A life of one-night stands, of fear and anxiety? *Shit.* Just when I think I can't get more fucked up I manage to top myself.

I pull on a simple black t-shirt and splash water on my face, trying to pull myself from this messed up headspace before I get to Vee. Reggie will smell the fear and anguish on me from a mile away, and then he'll send my ass home. Not to be an asshole, but because he doesn't want distracted workers. Anyone that isn't one hundred percent focused would piss off the Whitakers because it could put Rose at risk. Rose, who will have questions about Calluna and look at me all too knowingly. I let out another deep breath and walk to my door, pulling it open with plans to grab something to eat before heading to Vee. Anything to get out of this fucking house where I am ambushed by my thoughts.

I walk into one of the diners in town, Yes, Now Bob, and take a seat in one of the booths. I never used to feel comfortable coming to a restaurant and eating by myself. Now, I find myself never wanting company, but also, never wanting to be alone.

A waitress walks over to me and asks what I want, and I order the first thing I see on the menu—a burger and fries. I look up when I hear a loud yell.

"More ice cream, Bob!" a woman with dark brown hair yells as she sits at the counter with what looks to be a full bowl of ice cream. A sharply dressed man beside her chuckles, bringing a small teacup up to his lips. "Do you know what I'd like to do with this ice cream, Ford?" she asks the well-dressed man abruptly, getting very close to his face.

"I can only imagine, Sapphire," he replies with a smile.

"I'd love to slather it all over your cock and asshole, then lick you clean," she says sultrily, and it makes even my cock twitch just picturing the image in my mind.

"Let's wait for Bob, then we can leave together," Ford responds, his voice sounding considerably deeper.

"Mmmmmm," she moans, placing another large bite into her mouth. "A Bob and Ford ice cream sammich. Yes, now Bob!"

I draw my attention back to my own table, pulling out my phone to scroll through Screech. Nothing catches my attention, but I continue to scroll, wanting to concentrate on something other than the loud woman describing what she'd do to whom I can only assume are her mates with ice cream. The waitress returns, placing my plate in front of me and smiling widely.

"You're one of the bouncers at Vee, aren't you?" she asks, as she pours more water into my cup. I nod to her, forcing a smile on my lips.

"I've seen you there before. Will you be there tonight?" She asks the question while fluttering her eyelashes, like she's having some kind of attack, although I think it's meant to be flirty.

"Yeah, I'll be working tonight," I reply as I reach across the table to grab the ketchup, hoping she'll take the hint that I'm trying to eat and leave.

"I'm surprised your girlfriend wouldn't want to eat lunch with you before you have to head off to work. Unless she's working now too?" she pushes, and I force my eyes to not roll.

"No girlfriend," I answer curtly.

"What a shame," she says in a tone that doesn't match the words. I just nod, taking a large bite of my burger. "Maybe I'll see you tonight, I plan to head to Vee when I get off at eight."

I force another smile and nod, my mouth full of burger. She smiles back and turns on her heel, heading back to the kitchen. The food feels like gravel in my mouth as I continue to listen to the woman, that I've learned is called Sapphire, talk inappropriately to her mate. I slam money on the table and walk out, deciding that solitude is what I need. I move to the forest that borders the back of the restaurant, closing my eyes and concentrating on shifting. I feel the sharp prick as feathers and fur emerge from my skin, then I drop to all fours as I turn into a griffin.

Chapter 13

Calluna

I wake up and realize that I've slept most of the morning and afternoon away. The setting sun in my window shines directly into my eyes, and I rub my face, trying to wake up. I push the book away from me and hear it drop to the floor. *Shit*. I lean over the edge and begin looking for it, only to have my hand bit by Lina. She slithers away like a snake, then leaps up onto the dresser to curl up in a ball. "What the fuck, Lina?" I growl at another one of my misfit pets, throwing a small pillow at her and causing her to caw at me like a crow. I shake my head and get out of the bed, throwing my hair up in a more presentable ponytail and changing my clothes.

Rushing from my apartment, I pause and take a second to think about why I am in such a rush in the first place. I shake my head slowly, as if trying to rattle my brain around and get it to work. The pull I feel to leave my apartment is strong, and my time doing magic has taught me that you always follow the pull. I look at my cellphone to see if Lars texted about any issues at the store and sigh in relief when I see that my text messages show zero.

The sun has gotten so low in the sky that it is fast becoming dark, but I continue to speed walk down the street, still unsure of my destination but determined to get there. When I turn onto the street that my store lies on, I feel frustration until my feet take me to a different place. Black Moon Magick. I push the door open without a second thought and feel myself relax perceptibly once I get inside. I look around to see Falcar sitting in an armchair in the corner of the room, incense smoke billowing in small, wispy clouds beside him, a book in his hands. The bell welcoming me into the store rings quietly, which draws his eyes up.

"Calluna." He says my name like a greeting, and I cringe a bit.

"Falcar," I reply, avoiding his gaze and looking around his store.

He smiles at me, and even though he is clearly attractive, I find myself unnerved. "I knew you'd come back."

"Did you?" I ask with a frown. "Because I didn't."

"I didn't realize that your partner didn't know what you were," Falcar says, gently closing his book and setting it on the dark wood table beside him. "I'd assumed that you had shared that part of yourself with him. You seem close."

"He knows I have elven heritage, but that's all. Changelings aren't welcomed in the supernatural community, as you well know." The words leave my lips in a biting tone, and I take a deep breath to try to calm myself.

"Hmmm..." he hums, looking at me with a frown of his own. "You shouldn't be ashamed of your nature."

I squeeze the bundle of sage in my hand tightly. "We don't all live on the dark side so freely." I pause, gently setting the sage back down. "Has anyone else come in?"

Falcar walks closer to me, inspecting the sage before arranging them back in a line. "Would you appreciate me sharing your time here with others?"

"No, I don't suppose I would," I admit.

"Then why should I divulge the activities of others?"

A growl leaves my lips as I pivot on my heels. "Someone is cursing animals in town, and I'm trying to stop it. If you protect that kind of evil bastard, I can only assume that you're evil yourself."

He steps forward and is in my face in an instant. "Do not question me, little girl," he snarls into my face.

I eye him warily, until I see his face relax a bit and that stupid smile crosses his lips again. Frowning, I push him back. "I have been trying to remove the curses from them, but I never get it completely right. Something is always left over."

He turns away from me and walks over to a cabinet by the wall. "Well, it doesn't sound like you're a very good witch then, *changeling*."

"No shit." A sigh leaves my lips as I step toward him. "I just started this when the first cursed animal came to my store. My cat, Lina. Mine, because no one will adopt her. She came into the store with evil inside her. It radiated off her in waves and made me want to do horrible things. The woman that brought her in, an elderly woman that lived outside of town, she said that the cat made her kill her son. She gave me the cat, then turned herself in to the police. It was the strangest thing. The police found no reason to pursue anything having to do with the cat though. They said that the woman was crazy."

"How do you know she wasn't?" Falcar demands, looking at me like I'm foolish.

"Because I fucking felt it, too. I went home and found a

book that my grandmother had left me and did the first spell I could find. So now I have a cat that fluctuates between whatever fucking species she thinks she is at the time."

Falcar begins laughing like it's the funniest damn thing he's ever heard, and I glare at him. "I'm sorry," he says through belly laughs. "Are all the animals like this now?"

"No. Though, I do have a monkey named Jake with a very similar condition. But I also have a dog shitting glitter all over the damn place, a fucking guinea pig that loses all its fur every full moon, then starts feasting on other fucking rodents! There is a turtle that fucking explodes when he gets scared. Boom, all over the damn place. I'm becoming known for selling fucked up animals," I spit out.

"How do the animals come to you?" Falcar asks, barely suppressing another laugh.

"All the same. Dark as fuck." As I say the words, a shiver runs through me as I think back to how it felt each time another one of them would enter the shop. "There is another thing. A shifter, he was attacked the other night. Same black smoke." I rehash the night with Damian and Rhett, explaining everything I did.

"Here." He opens a cabinet and pulls out a large book and a few bottles. He walks over to another cabinet and grabs a small bag and begins to stuff herbs into it. He carries all the items to the counter and puts them in a plain brown bag like I'm buying porn or something.

"How much?" I ask, pulling my wallet from my purse.

"Nothing," he says, giving me that fucking scary smile again. "Let's just call it the start of a lucrative partnership."

"Why does it feel like I'm making a deal with the devil?" I ask as I slowly grab the bag before leaving the store, ignoring his laughter following me out.

Chapter 14

Rhett

Damian jumps up, barely awake, searching the room for predators when I move from the bed. I put a hand on his shoulder, trying to calm him. "It's okay. I just have to go to the bathroom," I say soothingly.

He nods slowly, looking me over carefully. "How are you feeling?"

"I'm okay, other than a full bladder," I say as I try to pull away again, so he smiles and lets me go. I walk out of the room, feeling strange on my feet as I step on the floor. One look at the clock tells me that we slept the whole day and into the night. I pee and return to my bedroom, smiling at the sight of Damian on my bed.

"What happened last night?" I ask, still worried about the events that played out. "You said that we'd talk about it when we got here, but I'm assuming we were both too tired."

"Someone cursed you. I thought you were going to die." He shivers involuntarily. "If it weren't for Calluna, you probably would have."

"What about the dog?" I ask. The image of the dog on the stone flashes through my mind, fear and pain lancing my chest at the memory.

"He didn't make it," Damian says quietly, his face masked in sadness.

"What? No!" I gasp, putting my face in my hands. "I need to see. I need to see him."

"See him? Rhett, I left him at Calluna's. He was dead shortly after we arrived."

"We need to go there." Jumping out of bed, I rush to the dresser and grab some clean clothes, not feeling up to shifting.

"It's late. We can go to the store tomorrow. Come back to bed," Damian insists, his eyes pleading with me, but I shake my head sternly.

"I need to do this, Damian." I stare into his eyes imploringly.

"Fuck," he grumbles, dragging a hand down his face. "Fine. Let me text Calluna first, make sure she's even awake."

"Text?" I ask with a quirk of my brow. "I didn't realize we were on texting terms with her."

"We aren't, I am. She gave me her cell number before we left her store, in case anything else happened with you." Damian shakes his head, looking down as he types out something on his phone. Odd, but I feel no spark of jealousy. Should I? Neither of us is truly gay, nor truly straight for that matter. We just are what we are. We want what we want, and right now, we want each other. He could leave me for a woman at any time. Could that woman be Calluna? Lost in my thoughts, I jump a bit when his phone makes the loud *ding*, indicating a text back.

"What'd she say?" I ask, feeling eagerness fill me.

"She said she's close to the store and that she'll meet us there," he says, typing out another message before pocketing his phone. When he looks back up, his eyes meet mine. "What?" he asks, looking at me questioningly.

"Nothing," I say, then pull him towards me and press my lips to his. "Let's go."

I find myself speed walking through town, and Damian is right there with me, step for step. "Where's the fire, Rhett?" he asks, continuing to keep up with my pace.

"I'm not sure," I say honestly. Is this all about a dog? A dog that I'd never seen before nor truly remember? Damian just nods and reaches out to grab my hand in his. I squeeze his strong hand in my own, feeling comfort in his presence. As we get closer to the store, I feel the urge to run, but I squash it down. I don't want to bust into the place like a maniac and scare her.

I see her in the window from the street, and it suddenly feels as if my chest could explode. She stands there in black leggings paired with a black tank top that has a cat on it giving the finger. Her hair is up in a ponytail, but long, blackish brown strands fall every which way, and I have the urge to push them behind her ear. Is this the woman I saw this morning while I was in a daze? I remember her being beautiful, but this, this kind of beauty makes me want to drop to my knees and cry. It makes me want to claw at my chest to remove the offending organ that beats far too fast, that aches at the thought of not being able to drag my fingers against her cheek or even to just speak to her.

Against my better instinct, I shift, and my small fox runs

towards the door of her store at a much faster speed than my human form could ever reach. She sees me and smiles, opening the door and letting me in. I begin to let out small yips of excitement as I rush around her feet. Damian walks in, an inquisitive smile on his face as he watches me bounce around. Unable to stand being in this form anymore and not being able to speak to her, I shift at once. My body moves from her feet to standing taller than her, looking down into her beautiful brown eyes.

"Calluna." Her name comes out of my mouth as a deep, hoarse growl, as if it hurts to say it.

"Hello, Rhett," she says with a sweet smile, then looks over to Damian. "Hi, Damian. Are you both okay?" she asks, the smile never leaving her lips. She looks to both of us in a strange way that makes my fox puff out his chest.

"You are mine," I growl out, flinching at the roughness of my words. That I would say such a thing to a woman I haven't even had a full conversation with is outrageous to me, but my fox chirps in happiness, pushing me on. Without a second thought, I grab her shoulders and pull her to me, smashing my lips to hers. She squeaks in surprise, her hands in fists on my chest, and then she suddenly begins to relax against me. She opens her mouth for me, so I slip my tongue inside to taste her, and she almost feels like an aphrodisiac. I let out a low growl and pull myself away, unwilling to allow myself to lose any more control.

When I back away, she looks at me, a dazed, almost drunken expression on her face. Then she snaps out of it suddenly. "What the hell?" she shouts, looking between me and Damian.

Damian's jaw is slightly ajar as he looks between the two of us, but I see the fire in his eyes. His head tilts to the side, and he breathes in deeply, twitching slightly as the air enters his lungs. He exhales slowly, and a word leaves his lips as the breath whooshes out.

"Mate."

Chapter 15

Calluna

"I'm sorry, what now?" I ask the two men that are looking at me like I'm dinner. With the way my panties have flooded with moisture, I would say that I'm A-OK with being their meal, even if my mind hasn't quite caught up. My chest still rises and falls quickly after that kiss that Rhett laid on me. That rough, passionate, hot as fuck kiss that has left my lips feeling swollen and delicious. I look over to see Damian looking at me in wonder and Rhett looking at me with pure, unadulterated lust.

"You're ours," Rhett says with a big smile as he takes a slow step towards me. I back up, putting my hand up to give myself a little distance so that my brain can function and I can form words. If he gets too close, I might resort to dry humping his leg, although I am anything but dry.

"Aren't you guys each other's?" I ask incredulously, my eyebrows raised and my voice squeaking a bit. "How could I be either of yours if you two are together?"

"Because you're ours," Rhett replies in the most

unhelpful way possible. I glare at him and turn to Damian, who seems to be as surprised by all of this as I am. Changelings do not have mates. There's none of that wacky shifter shit where you lay eyes on a person and *boom*.

Fuck it all, because nothing else seems to matter anymore but them. Nope, I've been pretty proud to come from a species that gets to use their own mind power, fuck you very much. But instead, I find myself drawn to both of these men in a way that I wasn't drawn to them before.

"Would you like to buy a ferret?" I blurt out the first words that come to mind.

"A ferret?" Damian asks, looking at me oddly.

"Sure. I'll buy anything. I'll buy it all," Rhett replies, and I glare at him again.

"I mean..." Damian rubs the back of his neck and looks at me uneasily. "Do you feel this? Any of this?" he asks, motioning between the three of us.

"No," I state resolutely, and Damian's face falls a bit. Rhett's smile just grows, and he steps closer to me.

"Bullshit," Rhett spits out, a wicked smile on his lips.

"Yes. Fuck, I don't know," I say without thinking again, just because I can't stand seeing Damian's face look sad anymore. What the fuck is wrong with me?

"So, we figure this out... Take it slow," Damian goes on, looking at me warily. Who hurt him so much that he feels the need to walk on eggshells about this?

Rhett growls softly. "Fuck slow! She is ours, our mate. It's killing me to not mark her right now." Apparently, Rhett is ready to just jump in headfirst.

"Mark me?" I squeak loudly, both hands coming up to cover my neck. I internally scold my vagina for clenching at his words.

"Don't worry about your pretty little neck, sweetheart.

I'm more of a tit guy myself," Rhett says with a soft purring noise.

A breathy squeak leaves my throat as I let out a breath of air. Damian grabs onto Rhett's shoulder, pulling him back and away from me. "Damn it, you'll scare her, Rhett."

Rhett turns to Damian and grabs the man's shirt, pulling until their chests slam together with a hard thump of pure muscle. Their growls fill the room before their lips crash together. "Don't think I'm willing to give you up," Rhett growls into Damian's mouth.

Well fuckity, fuck fuck. Fuck fuck fuck. I feel myself instantly panting like a dog as I stare at the men kissing and pawing at each other. Son of a bitch. I am barely refraining from stripping down so that I can feel their lips on me, on my body. Damian's hand slips down and under the waistband of Rhett's jeans, causing both Rhett and I to groan at the same time. The noise reminds the men of my presence in the room, and they break apart.

"I'm sorry," Rhett says abruptly, and Damian nods in agreement. "The urges I'm feeling right now are uncontainable. I am barely holding myself together. Tell me I'm not the only one?"

Damian shakes his head, his chest rising and falling with his deep breaths. "You're not."

"Nope," I relent, causing both men to smile at me. "Fuck fuck fuck. What is this? I wasn't supposed to have a mate, let alone two! I mean, I've always thought having multiple men was the way to go and hot as fuck, but mates? This is insane. Insane. Fuck fuck fuckity."

"You feel it too?" Damian repeats, staring at me in awe.

"Is that all you got from all that? Yes, I feel it. I want to rip the clothes off of both of you and have my way with you right here and now. I want to watch you fuck each other, and

I want to writhe beneath you both as you fuck me. I want you to fuck him while he fucks me, and every fucking combination we can come up with. I am so fucking wet right now, and the thought of allowing you to mark me or bite me or whatever the hell you fucking shifters do is both terrifying and sexy as hell." I squeeze my hands together to refrain from doing all the things I just said. To keep me from touching them or from touching myself. Fuck, I just want to be touched.

"Let's do that," Rhett says in a husky tone, his eyes dark with lust and an unmistakable bulge in his pants. A thought runs through my mind, of dragging my tongue against his length, and I unconsciously lick my lips.

"No," Damian says sternly, looking at Rhett. "We will do this properly. We won't take advantage of you when something you're unprepared for is altering your senses. We were raised with the knowledge that this could happen, we were told what the feelings are like, and although they are hard for us to contain, *we can*." He growls the last words, looking to Rhett. Rhett grinds his teeth together before nodding in agreement. "So for now, we'll go. We'll come back tomorrow when it's a proper time and we can speak about this like rational adults."

I nod my head slowly, my chest clenching at the thought of them leaving. "I think that'd be for the best," I say the words softly. Then, against my better judgment, I voice a question that is plaguing my mind. "Are you guys going to go home and fuck each other?" I ask, my voice squeaking again.

A dark, sultry smile spreads across Rhett's lips. "Fuck yes we are, darling. Although we do a wonderful job of turning each other on, know that our cocks will be that much harder at the thought of you. That we'll both be wishing it was your skin we were tasting, that it was you our cocks were plunging into. It'll be fucking wonderful and hot as fuck, but it'll be only half the explosion that will happen once we finally get to claim you as ours. Because, darling, when we take you, it will be everything." As he says the words, he moves toward me without me noticing, and I jump slightly as he slams his lips to mine again, tasting me like he said he wants to. *Fuuuuuuck.*

I let out a soft moan, leaning forward and chasing his lips as he pulls away, making him chuckle softly. Cocky motherfucker. Then Damian steps forward and places a small kiss on my cheek. "Tomorrow, Luna." His accent lilts the words, and I fucking melt.

I watch them both leave the store, and I can't help but stare at their asses. Then the thought of what they are headed to do flashes in my mind. Fuck, I should call them back. Say fuck it and let them ravish me right here in my own store.

Fucking balls, what is happening to me? I quickly walk to the doors and lock them, then flip off all the lights. I walk to the back of the store and lie back on one of the couches, slipping my fingers beneath my leggings and panties to dip one into my core and gather some of the wetness there. I bring it up to my clit and begin rubbing myself as I picture what must already be happening between Damian and Rhett. My head thrashes and my muscles tighten as one of the quickest orgasms I've ever experienced hits me with ferocity.

Fuck fuck fuckity fuck.

Chapter 16

Calluna

Walking into the store the next morning, I'm sleep-deprived, grumpy, and unbelievably horny. I spent all fucking night touching myself and never felt like it was enough. I swear I have carpal tunnel now. Lars greets me with a smile that quickly turns into a look of confusion.

"What crawled up your butt?" he asks, handing me a to-go coffee from Jewels Cafe.

"Bless you," I praise, then take a long drink of the coffee. "And *nothing* has crawled up my butt," I groan.

"Ahhhh, so you're sad about that?" he says with a small chuckle.

"About what?" I snap, eyeing him angrily.

"About nothing crawling up your butt...or one of your other orifices," he says, not even trying to contain his laughter. I just give him a small growl as an answer, since he isn't wrong.

I spent the whole night trying to figure this shit out, in

between flicking the bean, of course. There are many species that mate, and maybe changelings do too. Fuck, I don't know. I was raised by humans, like most changelings are.

When a dark elf and a fae have a baby—which is usually seen as an abomination to both species—the couple steals a human child in the night and replaces it with one of their own to keep the secret of their coupling. The human child is said to be given to the devil or some kind of fairy god, who fucking knows, and the changeling child is raised by humans. The child grows up believing they're human until they realize they aren't because they have wacky fucking powers.

Obviously, I gained all this knowledge from reading, as I know neither of my biological parents. When I started showing magical abilities, my human parents saw me as disobedient and evil—the bible thumpers that they were—and kicked me out. At fourteen, I began living on my own, mostly using the magic I learned to steal and manipulate. True to my nature, I suppose. That's how I got the money I needed to open my store. I always had a passion for animals due to their magical nature, and when I discovered Silver Springs was mostly supernatural, I decided to settle here.

"Tell me about mating," I say to him suddenly, needing to get all the information I can.

"Well, sometimes a boy likes a girl, birds and bees, you know. Well, penis-vagina, penis penis, vagina vagina, penis mouth, etcetera," he explains, laughing the entire time. I grab a tennis ball dog toy nearby and chuck it at him. He snatches it out of the air without issue and smiles widely at me.

"Shifter mating, asshole," I growl.

"Man, you really are grumpy today." He frowns slightly,

setting the tennis ball on the counter. "It's mostly hetero shit, but it happens from time to time with gay couples. I've obviously never experienced it, but from what I've been told, it's like a punch to the chest. Your world suddenly becomes all consumed by that one person or persons. As if they're the one thing holding you to the ground, they become your gravity and your oxygen. The thought of living without them hurts. The need to claim, to take, to make them yours is irresistible. Everything about them is perfect, even the imperfect parts. The attraction is so intense that seeing them feels almost like being electrocuted, but in an oddly good way. They're it for you. Everything you ever wanted, and everything you never knew you wanted."

A breath whooshes from my body as he finishes explaining. I look at him seriously. "You seem to know a lot about something you consider bullshit."

"The way my mom explained it to me always stuck with me. She was so sweet and innocent, maybe it's not like that for everyone. It just sounded so wonderful to me when I was a child." He sighs, then rolls his eyes. "Now, though, I'm more concerned about getting that dick." He winks at me as he pulls back into his natural demeanor.

The laugh is pulled from my body as a choked sound, and he looks at me curiously. "Why the sudden interest in mates, Cal?"

"No reason," I say softly, taking another drink of my coffee. I close my eyes as I feel the warm liquid settle in my chest. My chest that has been aching uncontrollably since last night. Will they come in today? They said they would. I keep my eyes closed tightly, remembering the kiss that Rhett gave me last night, and I squirm in my chair. I think of the looks in their eyes as they gazed at me, like I was the most gorgeous thing in the world. Like I truly was the oxygen they were breathing.

Fuck, all those things that Lars said. All those words that he's held on to since he was a child are exactly how I feel, and I don't know how to fucking handle it. I have mates? How the flying fuck do I have mates? Why didn't we realize this connection when I first saw them the night that Rhett was attacked? Did my magic somehow create this mate connection? Son of a bitch, what if I did this to them? To myself?

I'm pulled from my thoughts when I hear the door open. My eyes pop open, ready to help whatever customer has entered my store. I paste on my fake smile and stand, setting my coffee down. "Welcome to Bea—" The smile drops from my lips, and I pause as my eyes land on the two men that have completely consumed my thoughts for the past twelve hours.

"Good morning, beautiful," Rhett says, walking into the store as if he's exuding sunshine. His smile is cocky as his blue eyes zero in on me. The sun catches in his messy, sandy blond hair, making his skin look tanned and delicious. As he moves towards me, I notice how his muscles flex and move as he walks, giving me the irresistible urge to run my fingers over their hardness. Behind him walks Damian, and my breath catches again. The lightness of Rhett's features is in contrast to the dark brown of Damian's hair and beard. His hazel eyes shine as they reach my own, and his lips quirk into a small smile, almost like he's shy. His quieter nature intrigues me, as if he's the thoughtfulness to Rhett's brashness. They are truly yin and yang, complementing each other in the best ways.

"Good morning to yourself," Lars growls, his voice sounding husky.

"Larson, back off," I growl, using his full name to show how serious I am. I look over to him and see his eyes widen perceptibly as he looks to me and then to Damian and Rhett. He looks awestruck, double-taking between the men and myself. Then he regains his composure, and with a wide smile, crosses his arms.

"Now I get your questions." He chuckles, then winks at me. "I have to head to Willow's shop, anyway. We need more herbs. I'll be back. Don't do anything I wouldn't do," he sing-songs as he walks out the door.

His absence is immediately felt, and it's like the air in the room feels magnetized with just their presence. I can almost feel a string attaching them to me, pulling me towards them.

"Luna," Damian says as he gets to the counter that I'm still standing behind. He grabs my hand and brings it to his lips, kissing it softly. The way he says the end of my name, like a prayer, makes my knees weak, and I feel as if I could melt into a puddle on the floor.

"Good...good morning," I stutter, feeling my stomach clench in nerves. Who the fuck am I? I don't get nervous. I exude confidence. I take what I want, hard and fast. "How was your night?" I ask, wincing slightly as I remember Rhett's promise of what they'd spend it doing.

Rhett's smile is mischievous and dark at the question. "It was delectable." He says the words slowly, each one filled with meaning.

"When will Larson be back? We'd like to take you somewhere," Damian asks, pulling me into the depth of his eyes.

"Larson?" I squeak, staring at him in longing. "Oh, Lars. I don't know."

Damian chuckles as I make a complete fool of myself, and I try to shake myself free of this cloud that's hanging over me. *A cloud of motherfucking lust and horniness.*

"If I fuck you guys, will I be able to think straight again?" I blurt out, regaining a bit of my natural charisma.

Rhett cracks up, literally throwing his head back in laughter, and Damian just smiles widely at me as he holds back his laughter. "I know this must be strange for you, Luna. It probably doesn't help, but we also feel out of control and erratic."

"It does help, a bit," I reply, feeling myself relax slightly. "Fuck it, it's my store. We're closed until Lars gets back. I'll text him."

"Perfect," Damian replies, grabbing my hand in his and squeezing it slightly after I send a text off to Lars.

Chapter 17

Damian

The feel of her soft skin in my hand comforts me beyond belief. The shock of finding my mate still hasn't left me, it's like looking at the world with new eyes. I'm also pleased to find that my love for Rhett has not faded at all, even with the mate connection sparking. It's like my heart just got bigger instead of a piece being replaced from one person by another. She looks up at me shyly, which is complete whiplash from the first moment I saw her. The fieriness of her personality is still there, just lying beneath all the confusion she must be feeling about all of this.

Rhett walks on the other side of her, and I can see by the way his muscles are tense and how his hand flexes that he wants to be holding her hand too. To just be touching her in some way.

We talked about this last night, about giving her a chance to navigate through these unknown waters without us pushing her. Our animals scream to us to take and claim, but she wasn't built the same way. She needs time to adjust to what her life has become, to what it will be. There's no doubt in my mind that this will happen. She is mine. *Ours.* I'll be unable to let her go now that I've found her. It would kill me. Rhett was combative at first, insisting that once we claim her that everything will be fine. That finalizing the connection will make things easier for her, but I disagree. We can't force this on her, and after hours of fucking each other in every way possible, he eventually agreed.

Fucking Rhett has always been amazing. Although I miss the softness of a woman, it's something amazing to be completely unleashed. I never have to fear hurting Rhett. His body is hard and strong, so he can take everything I can give him. Last night, all the pent-up aggression of not claiming our mate and the unbearable lust led to a very long and pleasurable night. It did little to take the edge off though, as Rhett and I are both battling ourselves again today while in her presence.

As we get to the edge of town, near the wooded area near our home, we stop. Looking down at her, I smile. "How fast can you run, Luna?"

"Run? My ass wasn't built for running," she replies with a laugh, looking at us both warily. "Don't say we're running."

"Your ass was built for everything," Rhett growls and smacks the offending body part. I shake my head as Calluna jumps with a squeak.

"It was built for a lot, but *not* running," she jibes back, stabbing her finger into his side.

"We don't have to run," I tell her as I watch her relax a bit. "Rhett, grab your bikes."

She tenses a bit as Rhett smiles and runs over to his shed about a hundred feet away from us. "Bikes?" she asks carefully. "What do you mean bikes? Where are we going?"

"It's a surprise," I answer, squeezing her hand in mine. "Don't worry, I'll keep you safe."

She makes a tsk'ing noise under her breath as she looks over at Rhett, who begins pulling his dirt bikes from the shed.

I pull her with me as I walk towards the blue dirt bike that Rhett has set up in the grass, leaning on its kickstand. I release her hand, but not before pressing another kiss to it, then throw a leg over the machine and grip the handlebars. "Get on back, *mi Luna*."

She looks at me incredulously. "I'm not getting on that."

"Of course, you are," I reply, scooting forward a bit. The sound of Rhett's bike starting up makes her jump. He flashes her a smile before revving the motor a bit and flying into the wooded area, following the worn-down paths. "Better hurry, or we're gonna lose him. You don't want that cocky fucker to win, do you?"

"Win what?" she asks, biting onto her full lower lip and looking from me to the forest with unease.

"Hop on and find out," I tease as I lean forward to pat the seat behind me. I watch as she sighs, then she walks over and gets onto the bike behind me. I scoot back a bit, feeling her warmth behind me. "Hold on," I yell as I start up the bike, and smile as her arms wrap around my waist, holding herself close to me. *I could live like this forever*, I think as I kick the bike into gear, and then we fly into the forest.

I follow the path closely, slowing down a bit at the small hills I've memorized so that we don't ramp them as usual. I ease her into the feel of the bike beneath us, slowly building up speed until I feel her tight hold relax a bit. I see Rhett ahead and know that he must have stopped to wait for us as I assumed he would, not wanting to miss out on seeing Calluna ride with me. I feel her laughing behind me as we watch Rhett do a quick donut and speed through the underbrush and off the path to get behind us. I take her laughter as acceptance to speed up a bit, doing less strolling through the paths and speeding toward our destination. She tightens her grip on me once again, but her chest quakes with laughter as she watches Rhett weave around us.

"Beat him!" she yells into my ear, and I smile, pulling back on the throttle to gain more speed.

As we come up to the small pond in our clearing, I slow down, whereas Rhett speeds by us, skidding to a stop and throwing dirt and grass into the air. "Show off," I yell at him as he kicks the bike into park and sidles off of it.

"Don't be jealous of my skills." He brushes off his shoulders exaggeratedly, winking at Calluna. She releases her hold on me, and I immediately feel her absence, the urge to keep touching her strong. I watch as Rhett walks up to her and pulls her into his arms. "I don't do *slow*," he says the words in a deep, husky tone that makes me hard as I catch on to the innuendo. *Mi Luna* also catches onto the innuendo and smiles up at him, not pulling away.

"No, it doesn't seem that you do." She stands up on her tippy toes a bit, pressing her lips into his. He kisses her back, but doesn't push her as I know he wants to. *Good boy.* "Lucky for you, I don't do slow either," she purrs, causing heat to surface in his eyes and my cock to get perceptibly harder. They're both going to kill me, but it'll be the sweetest death.

"So, where are we?" she asks, turning to look around. Rhett releases her for only a second before pulling her body back into his arms, this time with her ass pressed into him.

"Just our own little slice of heaven," Rhett replies, eyeing me with a smile. "This has always been mine and Damian's spot, and we wanted to share it with you."

Her eyes widen, and she looks at me in surprise, so I

smile and nod at her. "That's really...that's really nice. Thank you."

"We want to give you time to adjust to this, but we also want to spend time with you. We can do this as fast or as slow as you want. We can give you time to adjust to this, we just ask that you let us be a part of that adjustment," I explain, sitting on a log near the pond and looking out at the water. She comes over and sits down next to me, her hand linked with Rhett's.

"Thank you for sharing this with me. I truly appreciate this," she says to me, looking at the area with a smile on her face. A smile that makes my heart feel as if it stopped. "It's so beautiful. How long have you guys been coming out here?"

"Together, a couple of years. I found it a few years back when I used to go on runs by myself, and then when Damian and I got together, I brought him out here. Now it gets to be *our* spot," Rhett says, scooting next to her on the log and squeezing her between us. I put my hand on her leg and feel her relax into me.

She nods her head. "So, you guys have been together for two years? How does that work?"

"It works like you'd think it would," Rhett replies with a laugh, but I understand her underlying question. How does it work with us and her? Will she be okay with our relationship being separate from hers, even if she's in the center of it? Can she mesh into our lifestyle, or will she not like the relationship that Rhett and I have established?

"How do you want it to work?" I ask her, fearing the answer, yet dying to have it at the same time.

She looks up to me, and I study her features, trying to decipher what she's thinking. "I don't want to split you up. If I thought that could happen, I'd leave right now."

Relief fills me, and I grin at her. "What do you think of integrating yourself into our relationship?"

"I don't know. Would you guys get jealous? Say I fucked Rhett without you, would that feel like cheating? Do you guys even want me?" She pauses, tensing slightly. "I mean, I know this mate connection is forcing you into this attraction you have for me. Forcing you to want to claim me, but if it wasn't, would you want to add me to the mix?"

"Beautiful, it's a lot more than instinct that's drawing me to you. Every single part of you calls to me. From your sassy attitude, to this shy demeanor I've just recently seen. Your plump lips and your voluptuous body that I can't help but put my hands all over." Rhett grabs ahold of her chin and turns her face to his, looking at her more seriously than he typically would. "Sure, the mating drive is fucking strong. Looking at you, smelling you, just even fucking thinking about you makes my cock hard as a rock, but it's you that draws us. We love each other, but there's still room in our hearts for you. You're ours. The fates and magic don't have shit to do with that. No, that's in here." He points to his chest.

"Who is this man speaking such pretty words?" I ask with a teasing smile, causing Rhett to blush slightly. "In two years, I haven't seen this gushy side of you."

"Fuck off," he growls at me, his eyes intense. "How do you feel?" he asks me, making my heart clench. The fact that the three of us can discuss this as rational adults makes me truly believe that this will work. Mate connection to hell, we can make this work.

"All that you said and more."

Chapter 18

Calluna

Thousands of emotions overwhelm me as I sit between these two men that have me squirming on the hard log below me. Not that I normally argue with a hard log beneath me, it's just not quite the one I am yearning for.

Having Rhett explain their feelings to me gives me whiplash. The intelligent side of me screams that I just met these men, and that this can't be real. The *gushy* side, as Damian put it, is screaming that this must work, because even in this short amount of time, I know that they're mine. These two men are mine.

"Enough heavy stuff," Rhett says suddenly, breaking into my thoughts. "Wanna skinny dip?" He raises his eyebrows and gives me a flirty smile.

"I'm more of a chunky dunker, myself," I reply with a laugh, feeling more comfortable with them.

"Call it what you want. If you're naked, I'm down," Rhett says, standing and removing his shirt.

"You don't have to get naked," Damian says, his hand rubbing my leg comfortingly.

"What the hell," I reply with a grin as I stand. I pull off my shirt, revealing my lacey red bra, and pull down my leggings to show off my matching red lace panties. I may have dressed in relaxing clothes today, but I dressed up in terms of my underwear. With the amount of horniness I felt all last night and this morning, I knew that if I saw them, I'd want to jump them, and I'm nothing if not prepared. I don't feel self-conscious of the stretch marks on my stomach or the fact that I'm exactly what I said earlier—chunky— because of the looks in their eyes. They eye me like it's their last meal and I'm a filet mignon, with their mouths slightly open and their eyes blazing with heat. I feel my core clench under their lustful gazes, and I look at them expectantly. "Well, am I in this alone?"

"Holy fuck, sweetness," Rhett gasps, causing me to smile at him flirtatiously. He grabs onto the waistband of his shorts and pulls down, and I realize that he's going commando. His thick cock springs from his shorts, hitting him in the stomach, and it's my turn to stare.

Holy shit. Mama, may I?

The sound of clothes rustling beside me pulls my attention from Rhett back to Damian, just in time to see his shirt come off. I marvel at his sculpted chest, having never seen his body before. I mean, I saw Rhett while he was cursed, and although I tried not to look, I definitely accidentally on purpose sorta looked. *Oops.* Damian's tanned skin has a small amount of hair on his upper chest, then a mouthwatering happy trail heading down to his perfectly formed V. His sweatpants sit low on his hips, and I watch with my breath held as he slowly pulls his sweatpants down, releasing his own hardened cock. *Holy fuck, are these men always commando or just today? Dear Maker, I want to find out that answer.*

"Stop ogling us and get the rest of your clothes off." Rhett comes up behind me, his finger gliding under the strap of my bra and causing chills to run through my body. His finger continues its trail down until it reaches the clasp at the back, where he pauses, asking for my permission. I nod, and my breathing becomes shaky as he unlatches the bra and slowly pulls the straps down my arms, unleashing my large breasts. "Now let's get in," he growls in my ear, giving me goosebumps.

He and Damian jump into the water, splashing the entire way like a couple of children. The cool water seems to sizzle as it hits my skin, and it feels like it's streaming with electricity from their looks and touches. I slip out of my underwear and run into the water behind them, and the water is up to my breasts before they catch sight of me.

"That hardly seems fair," Rhett says with a chuckle as he swims closer to me. The water is deep enough here to where I can't touch the bottom, so I kick my feet, keeping myself afloat.

I smile at him, feeling myself come out of my shell more. "Never said I played fair."

I'm starting to feel more comfortable with them after speaking with them about the...err, terms of our relationship. I've never been one to overthink things, usually jumping in headfirst and dealing with the consequences later, but I felt like this situation was too important to just YOLO that shit. I meant it when I said that I didn't want to destroy their relationship. I don't know if I'll feel jealous or if they will, but the way that Rhett described it, it felt right. We just have to jump in and see how it goes.

Damian comes up behind me, and I see that he's standing, fucking tall bastard. He grabs ahold of my waist and helps me stay afloat, giving my legs a rest. He keeps his arms extended straight out, not pulling me into his chest like I want him to.

"Is this okay?" he asks quietly, timidly. I answer his question by spinning in his hands and wrapping my legs around his waist, feeling my core press against him. It takes everything in me not to squirm against his hard waist, but I refrain.

"This is better," I say as I wrap my arms around his neck. "Does anyone ever come out here? I'd hate for us to get caught out here all nakey and shit."

"Caught doing what?" Rhett asks, lying back to float in the water, which puts his cock on full display.

"Well, caught chunky dunking, I suppose. Or in your case, caught with your dick straight in the air."

"No one else comes out here. It's public land but not used often, mostly because of our scents being all over it," Damian explains, his hands sliding down to grip me closer to him, and I squirm a bit. *Shit, I tried.* He groans at my movement, and I try to hold in my small smile.

"Like you peed all over it?" I ask, scrunching my nose as I imagine nature documentaries and male lions peeing all over trees around their area.

Damian laughs, and the sound is so freeing that I can't help but smile widely. He seems to be relaxing at the same rate as I am, a seemingly slower pace in comparison to Rhett, who seems to move one hundred miles per hour. "No, we didn't pee all over it. Just us being here so much has marked the area with our scents. Besides, meerkats scent mark with their fur."

"Right, that's true. I've seen *Meerkat Manor*," I say,

thinking back to the TV show about the meerkat family headed by a matriarch, Flower.

Damian chuckles. "Right. Well, those are mostly real meerkats."

"Mostly?" I ask, surprised. "Which ones are shifters?"

"Tosca. She was a student at Cambridge University and really submerged herself into the study. That's why Flower ousted her. Knew she wasn't a *natural*."

"I thought it was because she'd mated with Carlos and had pups when she wasn't supposed to," I say, because I obviously know too much about the show.

"You shouldn't believe everything you see on TV, even if it is a nature documentary," Damian teases.

"Stop that. I refuse to believe that any of it is rigged. Next, you'll be telling me *The Great British Baking Show* isn't authentic or that the people on *The Bachelor* aren't really in love."

He shrugs, and I audibly gasp. *Do not* mess with me and my reality shows.

"So, you know what I do, what do you guys do?" I ask, interested to know more about the men.

"I'm a counselor. I work at a small center in town, run by the county. Mostly children and teens," Damian explains, and I feel a few butterflies flutter in my stomach. He's been so methodical and sensitive to this whole situation. I can see him helping kids.

"And what about you?" I ask, turning my head towards Rhett. "Something dangerous, I assume. You seem like an adrenaline junkie."

"Ha!" Rhett barks, skimming his fingers along my arms. "Nope, I work construction. Man's work." He winks at Damian, who just snickers and rolls his eyes.

We continue to spend the day swimming and talking as I

get to know these men that are seemingly working their way into my heart. Rhett constantly finds excuses to touch both Damian and myself—grabbing me to throw me into the water like I weigh nothing, and using Damian as a shield when I try to splash him. He sneaks up behind me, placing kisses on my neck and grabbing my ass below the water, then swimming away quickly before I can smack him.

Damian begins to relax more as well, his hands slipping down to cup my ass when he holds me against him or dragging his fingers gently against the side of my waist and breasts. I work hard to keep my libido under control. I touch them the same way, but we all play it safe. I glide my hands against their sculpted chests, abdomens, backs, and shoulders. I revel in the feel of their hard muscle beneath my fingers, imagining gliding my teeth and tongue against them.

When Rhett grabs me and I wrap my legs around him, I feel the tip of his cock near my core, and I can barely hold myself together. Everything in me begs to slide down onto him. His eyes blaze in a way that shows his mind is in the same place. Instead, he presses one of the most passionate kisses to my lips, as my breasts press hard into his chest, and my nipples pebble from our connection. His tongue explores my lips, then delves into my mouth when I open it, allowing him to gain entry. I unconsciously squirm in his arms, my slick core dragging against his tip, making us both groan into the kiss. Damian swims over, drawing our gazes to him, and he kisses me sweetly. His kiss is in direct contrast to Rhett's rough kiss. These two men are yin and yang, night and day.

When Damian breaks our kiss, Rhett removes one of his hands from my ass and grabs the back of Damian's neck roughly, pulling him in for a kiss that destroys me. They kiss each other roughly, growls rumbling in their chests as they make love to each other's mouths. Rhett's cock twitches below me, and I find myself more turned on than I've ever been in my life. I've always enjoyed male on male porn, loved watching the roughness and the men bringing each other to orgasm. Something is just unbelievably sexy about muscle on muscle wrapped around each other. This...well, this is like my own personal porn viewing, and some of the sexiest I've ever seen. How could I be jealous of their relationship when I get to be a part of it? How could I be jealous of something that can be both beautiful and mind-blowingly hot as fuck at the same time?

I can't.

There's not one part of me that doesn't want this with my entire being. I want them together, and I want them with me. I want to integrate myself into this love and passion that they already share with each other. I want to become part of that love and passion too.

I want them more than I've ever wanted anything before.

Chapter 19

Calluna

When we finally pull ourselves out of the water, the muscles in my legs and stomach are burning. I can't remember the last time I swam an entire day. The sun has long since set, and the sounds of nightlife echo in the forest. Damian and Rhett both respectfully turn as I get dressed, giving me privacy that I really no longer need. A good deal of our swimming adventure involved my pussy being pressed against either Damian or Rhett's waists, but neither made a move to further a connection. Light touches here and there were all I got, and I'm starting to feel a little sexually frustrated. If they were just guys that I'd met at Vee, I would have fucked them both already, but this mate connection has seemingly slowed everything down. Ironic, huh? It's like this shit is too important to fuck up. I mean, if it's so destined, then fucking shouldn't screw anything up. Right?

"You seem to be thinking awfully hard. If you keep biting that lip any harder, you're going to bite it off," Rhett says as he lifts his hand to pull my lip from between my teeth. He drags his thumb along my sore bottom lip, then presses a tender kiss on it.

I lift my arms up and pull my wet hair into a bun on the top of my head, knowing that it's going to be a tangled mess later. My tongue drags across my lips, tasting him there and wanting more. "Maybe we go back to your place?" I say, feeling brave.

"Maybe we take you back to your shop before Lars has a breakdown?" Damian cuts in, eyeing Rhett warningly.

"Well, you're no fun," Rhett grumbles, and I grumble my agreement.

"Tomorrow, *mi Luna*," Damian says, dragging his thumb against my lips. "Tomorrow, we can take this further."

"Why tomorrow? What's so special about tomorrow?" I whine, and then let my tongue slip between my lips to touch his thumb, causing him to tighten his grip on my lip.

"Tomorrow is a new day. Another day that we can spend getting to know you better."

I eye Damian in slight annoyance but concede, nodding my head in agreement. "So, who is going to give me a ride home?" I ask, my smile coming back to my lips.

"That would be me," Rhett explains, smiling at Damian. "You got her last time."

Damian nods, kissing me before walking with me over to the bikes. Shit, I can't get enough of their kisses. I've never had the urge to just make out with someone for hours on end—at least, not since high school—but these men bring out that urge in me.

Rhett starts up his bike, and I throw my leg around the back, scooching up behind him. I have to say that the vibrations do wonderful things to my clit, wonderful things that I will have to work out on my own, apparently. I wrap my arms tightly around Rhett's abdomen, loving the feel of his hard muscles beneath my fingers. I flatten my palm against him to really get the feel, and his chest rumbles in response.

"Damian and his fucking reasoning," Rhett growls, causing me to giggle against his back. "Let's do this thing, beautiful." My breath comes out in fast bursts as we rush through the forest, Rhett taking things a lot faster than Damian did on the way out here. I was a bit nervous on the way there, worried about my weight on the bike with another person, but since neither of them seemed worried about it, it must be safe. We take each hill at such a fast speed that after hitting some of them, we fly through the air, causing my heart to jump into my throat as I scream out in excitement. This is fun as fuck, and I kind of want to try driving one myself. *Next time.*

When we get out of the thick forest and into Rhett's backyard, I expect him to stop and for us to walk the rest of the way to my shop. Instead, he just continues driving through his yard and onto the street in front of his house. He goes much faster than the speed limit, weaving in and out of cars, driving down the small side streets, and earning us some angry glares. The whole thing makes me feel like a teenager again, and I can't help the squeals of excitement that leave my lips as we weave through traffic.

I look behind us to see Damian following closely behind, shaking his head in disapproval but still with a smile on his lips. How did someone as wild as Rhett meet someone as calm and sensible as Damian? Is there a wilder side to Damian that I haven't seen yet? That thought fills my chest with excitement at how many layers that man must consist of. I can't wait to peel them all back.

Rhett takes the long way to my apartment, adding a few miles onto our course, but I can't find myself complaining.

The wind in my wet hair, my arms tight around him, and the adrenaline have me feeling on top of the world. We pull onto Main Street, and I see the lights of Vee illuminating the street as people crowd outside. My eyes drift towards the entrance and see the man I was looking for, talking to Reg. The sound of the dirt bikes' motors draws Landyn's vision towards us, and he freezes, his eyes burning into mine. His whole body tightens, and it feels as if time has slowed as I stare back at him. The same yet slightly different feeling I felt last night with Damian and Rhett floods my system, and my grip tightens around Rhett's waist.

What the fuck?

We continue to zoom by, and Landyn and Vee are now in the rearview mirror. Well, metaphorical rearview mirror, since I don't actually see one on the bike. Shit, are we even supposed to be driving these things on the road? We fly by Jewels Cafe and down a few streets, ending up at Beastie Besties. The lights are still on, and I can see Lars inside on his phone. He looks up at the sound of the bikes and quirks an eyebrow at me. I get off the bike and feel my legs vibrating slightly as I step back onto the hard ground. Rhett kicks the bike into park, and Damian pulls up beside us, doing the same.

"Is Lars going to be pissed?" Rhett asks, looking through the glass at the man in question.

"Probably," I reply uneasily. "I've really been a shitty boss lately. I need to hire someone else to help out in the store. Especially if I'm gonna keep being flighty as fuck."

"Do you plan to continue to be flighty as fuck?" Rhett asks with a wink.

I grin at him playfully. "I'm sure, if you have anything to do with it."

"Damn straight."

"Rhett, you idiot. We aren't supposed to drive these in town. We don't even have fucking helmets on," Damian growls, walking up to us.

"Settle down, old man. Nobody saw."

Damian shakes his head. "Nobody saw? You did a fucking parade through town! Twenty or so people were standing outside of Vee alone." He pulls me out of Rhett's arms and into his own. "Today was amazing, *mi Luna*. Thank you for spending the day with us."

I lean into him, loving the warmth of him against my cold body. "I had a lot of fun, but I really do need to hire some people if there are going to be any repeats. I should have done it long ago. It's been Lars and me for so long, I always thought we had everything handled."

"There are some teens that I counsel that may be interested in work. They can be a little rough around the edges, but would work hard."

"Fuck, that would be awesome. I couldn't pay much more than minimum wage, but I could take on a few if you want to send over some resumes." I immediately feel some relief at the thought of there being more help in the store potentially. Even something as simple as cleaning out cages and playing with the animals would be a huge weight off my shoulders.

"Darling, they're teens. Their resumes won't be much more than their names and addresses," Damian says with a laugh.

"Right. Well, if you think they'd be good, send 'em over," I reply with a shrug.

"Will do," he says, pressing his lips to mine again. This time, I take it a little further, pulling him closer to me and sliding my tongue against the seam of his lips until he opens them and allows me in. He growls quietly against my mouth, pushing his tongue against mine, tasting me and warring for control. When he pulls away, he bites my lip, pulling it with him as he goes.

"Tomorrow?" I ask as my chest rises and falls with my fast breathing.

"Tomorrow," he rumbles, squeezing me closer to him. "See you then."

Chapter 20

Calluna

"Well, if it isn't Ms. Hernandez herself, gracing us with her presence," Lars drawls as I walk into the shop, looking behind me to watch the guys speed off.

"I'm sorry, Lars, I fucking suck. Please forgive me," I plead, then stick my bottom lip out.

"Yes, you do fucking suck," Lars replies, squinting his eyes at me in accusation. "What is happening with you lately?"

"What do you mean?" I ask nervously. "I know I've been flakey. I feel so bad that I've ditched you so much lately. If it helps, Damian knows some teens that I can hire to help in the store."

"That will be a relief. But no, I'm talking about this." He motions up and down my body, and I look down, unsure as to what he is referring to. "This new person. Just the other day, I was begging you to go out with me, to do something other than just sit in your apartment. After agreeing, begrudgingly, you fuck Landyn, then start hanging out with two very sexy men that seem to be in a relationship with each other. Add in one of them being stark naked when I showed up yesterday morning, and then you making out with the other out on the front stoop. You are asking me about mate connections and spending the day with these two. I gotta say, I'm not sure what the fuck is happening to you anymore."

"I took your advice, and I'm expanding my horizons," I hedge, plastering on a fake smile. "You should be proud of me."

"I don't know whether to be proud or worried. Do you really think it is wise to get involved with a gay couple? Do you think they are your mates? Because if not, I can only assume that will turn out horribly for you."

I stiffen at his words. "I'll be just fine."

He looks at me disbelievingly, and it pisses me off beyond belief. "Sure, you will."

I turn on my heel and walk towards the door. "Everything is fine, Larson. Trust me. Can you lock up?"

"Lock up? Where are you going now?" he asks me incredulously as I pull the door open and start stepping back into the night.

"I need to go to Vee. I saw Landyn on my way over here, and I think I need to speak to him."

Lars' jaw drops, and he looks at me like I have a horn sprouting out of my head. "Who the hell are you?"

"I'm fucking Calluna, new and improved. See you tomorrow." I give him a wave before I let the door close and begin walking toward Vee, really wishing I had my own dirt bike right now.

The night air is chilly, and part of my hair is still wet—that area near your hair tie that never dries completely, you know the place. I hold my arms together across my chest, not thinking about how I'll look showing up in my comfy clothes to a nightclub. Especially when my goal is to talk to one of the bouncers that I fucked the other night, who just saw me drive by on the back of another man's bike. *Talk about a fucked-up situation.*

The walk takes less time than I thought it would, mostly because I'm speed walking and I feel like I'm being dragged by that stupid invisible magical string. Fucking magical strings everywhere, pulling me from dick to dick. It seems like a weird thing to complain about, but I swear I'm getting whiplash. Or maybe dicklash.

As I get closer to Vee, I see that most of the people standing outside earlier are gone, the line has considerably shortened, and Reg is standing there with his fucking clipboard. What the fuck does he need a clipboard for?

"Hey, Reg," I grumble, ignoring the protests of the people in line that I walked around.

"Well, if it isn't the lovely Calluna. Nice to see you, *again*," he says, emphasizing the last word knowingly. "Loverboy is inside."

"Loverboy?" I ask, quirking a brow at him. "If you want his cock, lemme know and I'll back off. It's a nice cock, but I can find another."

"Mmmm," he hums, giving me another stupid smile. Damn, I'm grumpy. "It seems like you already found a couple others. But no, Landyn's cock is not for me. *Sadly.*"

"Can I go in?" I question him, already walking towards the door.

"Of course, my lady. Your cock awaits," he says with an exaggerated bow as he holds the door open for me.

I give him a sassy nod of the head and raise my brows as I walk into Vee. Lights immediately flash into my eyes, and I squint them as I allow my gaze to move across the room. A Chance the Rapper song blasts from the speakers, and people are gyrating all over the dance floor, but I have eyes for only one man, and currently, he seems to be hiding. I weave between people, making a beeline to the bar where I see my favorite bartender serving drinks with a fumbling Sebastian. Dean sits on a barstool at the end of the bar, watching Rose with heated eyes.

"Hi, Rose!" I yell, then lean over the bar so she can hear me but others can't. "Have you seen Landyn?"

"Yes, I saw him a while ago towards the back by the private rooms. Back for more?" she says with a grin and a knowing look in her eyes. *Freaking Reggie and his big mouth.*

"Something like that. Thanks." I smile at her, then walk away, nodding a greeting to Dean and Sebastian as I go.

Chapter 21

Landyn

I felt her when she entered the room. Literally felt her in my fucking bones, and her scent instantly flooded my nostrils. *What the fuck is she doing here?* I immediately make my way to the back, deciding that this area will be my next walkthrough. I'm working tonight, and I can't skive off again. Even if Vee has mostly returned to a safe place of business, I always try to stay vigilant. I care about this bar and the people in it, enough to not let my guard down. Even when a walking distraction in skintight leggings and a practically see-through white t-shirt walks in.

Seeing her earlier tonight on the back of that dirt bike felt like a punch to the gut, and not in a jealous way. I mean, there was definite jealousy there, which is an oddity in itself. I do not get jealous. No, the punch to the gut was something else. Like an irrational need to grab her off the bike and plow into her, right there on the street. An urge to drop to my knees in front of her and beg her to accept me as hers. To let me worship the ground she walks on, to worship her body in every way possible. This is obviously a lot more than some good pussy.

Mates, a little voice screams in my head. *She is your mate. Take. Claim. Mine.*

A growl escapes my lips as these thoughts spin in my brain. How in the fuck is someone who I just fucked a few nights ago my mate? Why didn't the mate bond kick in then? I clench my hands together, stress overriding my emotions. I can't have a mate. I don't deserve one. I'm too fucked up.

Too soaked in my own thoughts, I don't notice she has found me until I turn to leave the room and our eyes connect. *Fuck it.* The words flash through my mind as my feet move of their own accord in a beeline towards Calluna. Our lips crash together so hard our teeth clack, our hands roughly grabbing at each other.

"Room?" she asks, her voice breathy, and I nod as I grab her hand and pull her towards our room—the room we used last time. When we get inside, I slam the door shut and push her body against it roughly. My fingers graze over the handle, flicking the lock in place without skipping a beat. Her fingers grasp the bottom of my shirt and pull it off me in a rush, then she slams her lips back to mine once it is pulled over my head. I grab ahold of her leggings and underwear, pulling them both down at once and allowing her to kick them off. My fingers immediately find her core, and I rub through her slickness, growling in anticipation.

"So, fucking wet for me," I boast as I slide my fingers inside her, then remove them and stick them into my mouth. "Delicious." Her eyes darken at my words, and I grit my teeth as I try to hold myself together. "Onto the bed."

She nods her compliance and scoots backward until the back of her legs hit the edge of the bed. She sits down, and I grab her shirt and pull it quickly over her head, then reach back to unclasp her bra. Her breasts bounce out of the red lace bra that was restraining them, and her dark pink nipples harden under my gaze. I lean forward and graze my teeth over the hard bud, rejoicing in her gasps. Moans of pleasure escape her lips as I lean her further down on the bed and crawl on top of her, all while swirling my tongue around her nipple. My fingers move back to her core, and I slip two inside of her, wrenching a loud moan from her lips.

"Landyn, I need you," she purrs, but I shake my head in defiance. No, I want to play with her for a bit longer. I want to taste more of what is mine.

She leans up on her elbows and stares at me as I make my way down her body, placing kisses along her stomach to the patch of hair at the apex of her thighs. When I finally reach my destination, I drag my tongue across her seam, then stop at her clit to swirl my tongue. Her fingers immediately fly to my head and hold me in place as I tease her sensitive bundle, alternating between licking and sucking. Her legs begin to quiver, and her fingers dig into me as I slide two of my fingers inside her, sawing them in and out of her tight pussy. I suck her hard at the same time that I curl my fingers, hitting her g-spot, and she spirals. Her thighs tighten around me as she rides out her orgasm on my lips, and I lick up every drop. When I sit back up and meet her eyes, I feel that same tugging sensation inside me, demanding that I claim her. That I make her mine. I push the feelings down, edging closer to her as I stroke my painfully hard and swollen cock. The bulbous head feels as if it could burst, and there is a large amount of pre-cum on the tip. This is not going to last long.

But I have forever.

I shake that thought from my mind as I rub the head of my cock through her folds, teasing her clit a bit more. Once

I find her entrance, I slam home with no preamble and groan as I bottom out. She chokes on a sob as I pound into her, her nails digging into my back. She moans my name over and over as she writhes beneath me.

Mine.

Mine.

Mine.

The mantra chants in my head with every thrust, and I feel my hands half shift into talons and rip them through the bed. I growl and whip my head, trying to keep control of my beast. My griffin is begging to be let out. To chase her and make her beg for me.

"Landyn, I'm close. Harder, Lan. Pleeeease—" she moans huskily, tears in her eyes. I give her what she wants, fucking her within an inch of my life, and she takes all I have to give gladly. I look down at her to see her skin has paled, her eyes have changed to an eerie black, and her ears have lengthened to a point. She looks up at me like I'm the gravity to hold her in place, that she sees my monster and welcomes him with open arms. That her darkness would forever embrace mine. I roar my climax as I feel her explode.

"Mine," I growl, my voice sounding inhuman and my heart feeling as if it might burst. Her mouth drops open as she looks at me in surprise, her features returning to what I recognize. "You are mine, Calluna."

Chapter 22

Calluna

"What?" I ask, looking up at the man above me. "I—I don't understand."

"You're my mate, Calluna," Landyn says matter-of-factly, his softening cock still inside me. "I don't understand why I didn't realize it before, but it's clear to me now. You're mine." His face looks as if he's torn between resolution and pain. *Pain.*

I knew you had a thing for broken animals, but not broken men.

Lars' words echo in my head as I gaze up at a man that looks as if he's being given the whole world, only for it to be immediately taken away. The words are caught in my throat, as if they are surrounded by peanut butter. I can't swallow them, and I can't force them out. They're just stuck. His face drops, and he pulls away from me to sit on the edge of the bed. "You don't feel it."

"No. No—I do," I say, pulling myself up and wrapping my arms around the back of him. "I just don't understand why this just kicked in tonight. Or why you look like someone gave you a present and shot your dog simultaneously."

"I'm no good for you, Callie," he groans and rubs his hand against his face. "I'm not good. I can't make you happy."

"What?" I ask, straightening up behind him. "What are you saying?" My voice cracks, and my heart drops into my stomach.

He continues to stare down, shaking his head. "I can't do this. You deserve someone better for a mate."

"How did we get here, Landyn? You were just claiming that I'm yours, saying that I'm your mate, and now what? You changed your mind?" I feel my chest clenching, and my throat burns with unshed tears.

He turns towards me, and his face looks completely devastated. "Calluna, do you know what I did to people? I captured and killed vampires. I tortured them, and I remember it all. My hands are stained with the blood of innocents."

"What are you talking about?" I shake my head, touching his shoulder gently. "That wasn't you. Rose said that Shani manipulated you."

"I almost killed Rose. I captured her, Sebastian, and Reg. They should have fucking killed me." He puts his face in his hands, and his chest heaves as sobs wrack his body. "Even if she did manipulate me, why would you want someone with such a weak mind? How can I protect you as your mate, if I can't even protect myself?"

"Landyn, this is stupid. I don't need someone to protect me. I only need *you*. You said it yourself—we're mates."

"I think you should go, Calluna," he says, his voice strangely flat.

"Landyn, stop this." I clench my teeth together until it hurts, refusing to cry.

"Go," he grates out again, coldly. I stand up from the bed and grab my clothes, then pull them onto my body. I look over at him, and he's just sitting there with his face in his hands. After a sharp intake of breath, I open the door and walk back into Vee.

I push through the people still busy having their drunken fun and dancing in the strobe lights. Their bodies move almost robotically as I push through, and I feel as if I'm being suffocated by them. Everyone feels too close, too loud. I shove faceless bodies out of my way, the exit in sight. As I draw closer, I see Reggie standing up straight and gazing over the crowd with his hands folded in front of him, looking as intimidating as ever.

"Calluna. Find your man?" he asks with a knowing smile.

"Yeah, I found him. He needs help, Reggie, serious help," I say, barely holding in the tears.

Reg's face hardens, and he lifts his sunglasses to look at me closely. "What happened? Did he do something?"

"I've got to go. Tell Rose I said sorry that I couldn't stay." I push past him and out into the darkness. Once my feet hit the pavement, I start running down the street, needing to escape this place.

"Calluna!" Reggie yells out the door and into the night, but I ignore him, wanting nothing more than to be alone right now.

I only run for about a block, then stop because I'm not built for running. I walk towards my house, panting from exertion and begging the tears to wait. Just a couple more blocks. Almost there. Please, just don't cry.

Once my hand grabs onto the handle of my apartment

building, I can no longer hold in the tears. A sob rips from my throat as I dig in my purse for my keys, knowing better than to bother with the elevator that never works.

"Need me to fucking kill someone?"

I look up to see one of my neighbors, Juniper, staring at me and looking completely serious. "I-I–" I stutter as more tears come. When did I become this punk assed bitch? Crying over a man? Even if it does feel like he ripped my heart from my very chest and ground his damn boot into it.

"I have these new spelled dildos. Just say his name, and I can send them straight to him. They'll fly straight through the air at him in a swarm, like the flying monkeys in *The Wizard of Oz*, and slap him right in the face. If he really fucked up, I could add in some extras." She smiles at me, placing her hand on my shoulder. "Just say the word."

"I'll get back to you. Right now, I just need quiet."

Juniper frowns, then nods. "You know, I had this book that I think would help you out right now. But I gave it to someone else."

"A book?" I ask in confusion.

"Yeah, a stupid romance book. It had some interesting quirks though."

"Wha—" My breathing becomes quicker, and I look towards the stairs. "I gotta go."

"All I need is a name! Then flying dildo monkeys!" she yells after me, and I just know that her crazy ass is serious. Maybe I'll take her up on it, but first I need to get to that book.

I bust into my apartment and I'm immediately greeted by barks and other random noises, but I run straight to my bedroom and start crawling on the floor. Jake comes up behind me and gets onto my back, sitting on me like we're playing horsey.

"Jake, get the fuck off!" I spit out, getting on my stomach to look under the bed. I see it lying there, open with its cover face up. "There you are!" I yell, just as Jake scuttles under the bed and pulls it out of my reach. He begins giggling like a mix between a hyena and a monkey, bouncing it in front of my fingers tauntingly.

"Jacob Black, you bring me that book or no supper!" I yell, completely bluffing. I pound my fist on the floor, and he immediately begins imitating me. An idea hits me, and I start banging both fists on the ground until he starts to do the same, dropping the book. With one quick swipe, I reach out and snatch the book away from him, fumbling for it before he can get his grubby little paws on it again. "Ah-ha!" I boast, and he begins hissing at me like a cat.

I look over the book more closely and flip through the pages. I run over to my cabinet, keeping the book in my hands and my eyes on Jake, and grab some of my crystals and candles. I set them up in the way I remember doing before and lay the crystals on the top of the cover. I close my eyes and concentrate, feeling the small ball of magic ignite in my chest. "Reveal," I say quietly and open my eyes. It feels insane that I didn't see it before, that I didn't feel it before. Magic radiates off the book in waves. I stare at the color of the magic and grab a spell book off my nightstand. *Love.* Someone spelled this book. I read it and–

"Oh god," I say quietly, the realization moving though my body. *This book, this book did this.*

Chapter 23

Rhett

I wake up, and I'm practically bouncing. "Damian! Wake up! Let's go!"

He groans and rolls over, picking up his phone and looking at the time. "What the hell, Rhett? It's not even eight."

"I want to stop by Jewels Cafe when they open, get some coffee for Calluna, and meet her at the shop when she gets there."

He smiles at me sweetly, rubbing his eyes. "You're too cute."

I shove him, then lean down and kiss him. *I am cute.* "I'm excited, okay? Yesterday was amazing. I just want to see her. To kiss her."

"You're like a lovesick teenager," he says to me, smiling and shaking his head. "Besides, I have to work today. I have a few appointments, and I told Calluna that I would send some of my kids to her to help her out in the shop."

"Good," I say, smiling even wider. "More help in the shop means more free time for her."

He stands and walks towards the bathroom, yelling over his shoulder, "I don't expect you to wait for me."

"Wasn't planning on it!" I yell back as I quickly pull on some clothes, then run into the bathroom behind him to brush my teeth while he showers. "See you later, babe!" I say, putting my head around the shower curtain and taking a peek at his tasty ass as I do.

"Tell her hi for me." He grins, noticing my gaze and winking at me.

I walk to my garage, open it, and pull out my motorcycle. Maybe I can talk her into going on a ride with me. She seemed to like the dirt bike, maybe she'd like the bigger version even better. I put on my sunglasses and throw my leg over my beautiful black baby, then start her engine, living for the sound of her purr. I fly down the streets and get to Beastie Besties in no time, leaving my bike parked out front and walking to Jewels Cafe, as there is no way I can carry coffees on the bike. I get there quickly, run inside, and grab three coffees—one for me, one for Calluna, and one for Lars. Nothing wrong with getting in good with the bestie.

As I get back to the shop, I see that the 'open' sign is now facing the outside, so I walk up to the door, juggling the coffees as I walk inside. "Good morning, beautiful," I say as I walk in and find myself alone with Lars.

"Why, thank you. I have to say, you're really growing on me," Lars says with a devilish smile. If it weren't for Calluna and Damian, I would find his roguish good looks and charm attractive.

"No Calluna yet?" I ask, walking over to him and handing him one of the coffees. "I wanted to surprise her."

"Thanks." He raises the coffee to me with a nod before

taking a big gulp. "No, she isn't here yet. To be honest, I half expected her to be with you guys, though she did go to Vee last night."

"Vee? Really?" I reply, a twinge of jealousy roaring through me. "I wonder why."

"Not a clue. Said something about a 'new and improved fucking Calluna' and left. I have no idea what's up with her lately," Lars says thoughtfully.

I sit there with him and wait for over an hour, eventually getting up and playing with a variety of animals, as well as helping Lars clean cages and feed the animals. I can't understand where she could be, or why she hasn't at least called Lars. Fuck, I don't even have her number.

I pull out my phone and send Damian a text, asking for her number, and he texts back immediately with her digits and another text asking if she's alright. I text him back, telling him that she probably just overslept, then open a new message to text her.

Me: I hope you like cold coffee.

Beautiful: Cold coffee? Who is this?

Me: Your foxy lover ;)

Beautiful: Rhett?

Me: Of course, do you have any other foxy lovers? Now get your pretty ass to your shop so I can surprise you with cold coffee and my presence.

Beautiful: I'll be in soon :)

I slide my phone back in my pocket, a smile plastered on my face.

"Is the princess planning to show up today?" Lars asks, obviously seeing my smile. "Or are you texting Prince Charming?"

"Why don't I get to be Prince Charming?" I ask,

pretending to be insulted. "But yes, she said she'll be in soon."

"Damian just seems more charming than you." He smiles at me, then pauses, looking at me carefully. "Is she your mate?"

"What did she tell you?" I ask, curious as to why Calluna hasn't shared this with her best friend already.

Lars frowns. "Not much. Asked me a lot of questions about mates around the time you two showed up. Is it both of you?"

"Yes, it is."

"Don't hurt her. I know that this mate bond is drawing you to her, both of you. But you and Damian are together. I can only assume this will end badly." He continues to frown at me, his body rigid.

I shake my head. "We want her, both of us."

"You can't stop being gay. You're just going to get her all tied up in this and then realize that you and Damian can't do this anymore."

I slam my fist on the table, stirring up some of the animals in the room. "That isn't how this is going to end up."

I look at him and see his rigidity, his fists clenching and unclenching. His jaw is tight as he grinds his teeth together. I don't let my eyes leave his, glaring at him with all my intensity and showing him how serious I am about this. He knows nothing about Damian and me, or about our relationship with Calluna. The bell rings suddenly, indicating that someone has entered the shop, but neither of us pulls our attention away from the other.

"What's going on here?" Calluna asks, her voice sounding raspy to my ears. I look over to her and see that her eyes are puffy and she looks exhausted. Her hair is in its usual messy bun, and she's looking at us both in confusion.

"I was just letting foxy-boy here know the lay of the land," Lars says with a fake smile plastered on his lips.

"Oh, I'd love to hear all about the lay of the land. Especially in regards to *my* land," Calluna spits out.

"It's nothing, beautiful. Here's your coffee that was hot an hour ago." I hand her the cup from Jewels Cafe and smile at her warmly.

"Thank you, Rhett. I'm sorry that I ruined your surprise, but I really do appreciate it. It was sweet," she says with a small smile. I push her bangs from her eyes and behind her ear, keeping my hand on her cheek. She smiles up at me, then pushes onto her toes and places a kiss on my lips.

"I do have to run somewhere really quick." She bites her lip as she looks up at me. "I'll be quick, I promise."

"Do you want me to come with you?" I ask, my brow creasing in concern.

"No, I'll just be a bit." She looks over to Lars and points at him, her eyes squinting into a glare. "You be nice. Damian should be sending those kids over soon, hopefully. I'll be back beforehand, but if not, show them the ropes."

"Aye-aye, captain," Lars says with an exaggerated salute, causing her frown to deepen before she walks back out the door.

Chapter 24

Calluna

My annoyance flares as I exit my shop. The freaking nerve of Lars is outrageous, trying to warn off Rhett. He acts like he wants me to do shit, then when I start doing shit, he gets all huffy. Fucking men. After my night with Landyn, the last thing I need is another huffy man, especially one that I'm not even getting the joy of fucking from.

Anger continues to pulse in my veins as I cross the street, barely taking the time to look both ways. My eyes zero in on Black Moon Magick, and I pick up my pace, ready to burst into the store and show Falcar the book. If anyone could tell me what kind of magic the book holds, it would be Falcar. I push open the door, and the bell rings, but I don't see anyone around.

"Falcar?" I announce my presence as I survey the room. The sounds of humming draws my attention, and I begin walking towards the back of the store, listening carefully. It almost sounds as if magic is being done, so I step gently, trying not to disturb Falcar.

I peek around a curtain that blocks the back room and see two men standing over something black, their hands interlaced and their eyes closed as they mutter words. The other man is Falcar's direct opposite, his hair midnight black to Falcar's snow white and his skin golden in contrast to Falcar's olive. From there, the men begin to exhibit similar features in their tallness and hard-muscled bodies. Their square jaws hold a harsh line that gives them a regal appearance. Their thin lips pause their movement as a soft gasp leaves my lips when my eyes zero in on the object in front of them. A raven lies on its back, its wings spread out and motionless—dead. Black smoke wafts from its beak, creating odd shapes above its lifeless form.

Within seconds, the second man is in my face, staring me down with dove grey eyes. He spits foreign words at me, and I find myself pushed against the wall with a force I've never felt before. I squeak out a small noise, unable to speak.

"Nelcar. Enough," Falcar barks, and I crumple to the ground.

"It's you!" I growl, pulling my bag closer to me. "You're the one torturing animals. You're the one cursing them."

"Don't be ridiculous, little girl." The one called Nelcar stares at me frostily. "Do not speak of what you know nothing about."

I turn to run from the room, my stomach knotted, when I'm frozen in place. "Release her, Nelcar. Let her go!" Falcar demands of him. "We cannot hold her here, brother."

Brother. Rage flashes through me as I think of how big a fool I am. Trusting, even if feebly, in an unknown man, feeling a bond over dark magic, believing his words that the distinction between light and dark magic was just an illusion. That my darkness didn't mean badness. These men are the reason I embraced my darkness, the reason I turned to dark magic, and the reason that my soul has probably become tainted. My muscles relax as Nelcar releases his magic, and I rush out of the store, squinting in the brightness of the sun. I look around, unsure where to go. To the cops? Back to my store? What could I do against two men that have such power? A man that was able to stop me twice with his magic?

"You shouldn't be here," a voice growls at me, and I jump in fear, swinging around and expecting to see one of the high elf brothers followed me out. Instead, I find myself face to face with a Herculean sized man with a scowl and large black wings. Feathered wings. "What is your name?"

"Excuse me?" I squeak out, my mouth feeling dry. I can't help but observe his broad shoulders and taut chest. Warmth pools in my stomach when our eyes meet, and I find myself being pulled towards him. I look up, my hands on his muscular chest as he glares down at me. "I'm Calluna."

"Mate," he demands, searching my face as if angry with what he sees. "You cannot be my mate, there is darkness within you."

I freeze in his arms and look up at him as anger crashes through me. I shove him, releasing myself from his arms. He takes a threatening step towards me, and I thrust out my hands, black electricity shooting out of my fingertips and into his chest. *Well, that's new.*

"My mate will not be seen at a place such as this. Come, I will take you to my home," he growls in a caveman-like manner. A switch in me flips, and I'm seething.

"Not fucking happening!" I shake my head fast, anger

flowing through me. The electricity I felt before buzzes in my fingertips. "No. This is too much."

"Don't be hysterical. Come with me, now."

I point at him with every muscle tensed as the black electricity sparks from my pointed finger. "Let me get this straight. I have two fated mates that are fucking each other, one that's so fucked in the head that he's rejected me, and now you. A fallen angel that's pissed that I may or may not be practicing black magic? Nope! Not today, Satan. Not today."

His upper lip twitches as his muscles shudder. "Satan? You misunderstand me."

"No, you misunderstand me. This is not the fucking day to be fucking with me." I stomp my foot, irritated with myself for making such a childish move. I flick my fingers at him, my eyebrows raised. "Move along, Uriel."

"Uriel? That is not my name." He looks at me questioningly, like I'm some kind of puzzle he can't figure out. Like he truly believed that I would buy into the caveman trope and allow him to throw me over his shoulder and take me back to his cave.

"I'm sorry, Raphael? Gabriel? Michael? You'll have to forgive me, I'm not all that knowledgeable when it comes to religion. Now, if you'll move aside, Judas, I have somewhere to be." I push past him, deciding to make my way back to my shop. I need to wrap my head around all this. *Too much fucking information.*

"Judas was not an angel, and you cannot leave. You are mine."

"Let's get one thing straight, Castiel. I do whatever the fuck I want." I watch as his jaw goes slack, and he cocks his head at me in curiosity.

"I will accompany you then," he states, walking beside me.

"Fucking Maker," I mutter while grinding my teeth.

"It's actually Elias."

I ignore him, walking quickly, but he keeps up all too easily. I look around and laugh to myself at the ridiculousness of this entire situation. If it weren't for the wards of this town, then the women that are eyeballing him—due to him being shirtless—would be picking up their jaws from the ground at the sight of his wings. They're huge, his feathers as inky black as the hair on his head. A light scruff of matching black hair covers a jaw chiseled enough to make the strongest woman weep. His tawny skin covers a body that's ripped like a freaking god. I push into my store and find myself greeted by Lars, Damian, and Rhett's curious gazes.

"Oh great, you're both here. These two lovebirds are Rhett and Damian. They seem to think that in addition to each other's dick that I'm the bee's knees. You guys, meet Gabriel, a fallen dick that can't get up."

Rhett barks a laugh, and Damian smiles widely, causing his eyes to crinkle. "I'm sorry, a what now?" Rhett asks around strangled laughter.

"It's Elias. I'm an angel. She is mine," Elias growls, and I roll my eyes at him. I've been on board for this whole mate thing so far. I found myself falling hard and fast for Rhett and Damian, as well as completely okay with their relationship and how I would fit into it. Then, I found myself in Landyn's arms and began to experience feelings of more than just lust for him, before he decided to crush me. Now this? It's getting to be a bit too much, so pardon me for feeling a bit manic.

Rhett's lips thin as he eyes Elias carefully. "Okay, caveman, settle down. She's ours."

"This is so not what I meant by living a little, Cal," Lars says edgily, looking around the room as if he's enjoying the show. "You always did take things to the extremes though."

"Who are you? Another mate?" Elias growls, stepping closer to Lars and eyeing the bear shifter suspiciously.

Lars puts his hands up in innocence, backing away with a smile. "Nope, just the gay best friend. On that note, I'll go give the newbies an introduction to the store. Try not to scare them, okay?" he says, and I then notice the three teen boys sitting on the couches in the corner, eyeing us all with what looks like intrigue. A slightly chubby blonde girl sits beside them with a smile on her face. *Well, at least they don't scare easily.*

"I'm so sorry for my behavior. I'm Calluna Hernandez, and I own the shop. I'm so happy you guys will be joining us!" I try to sound enthused and plaster on an overeager smile. "I promise that I'm usually less intense."

I look over at Rhett and Damian, who are trying to hide smiles, and sigh deeply. "I did say less."

Damian shakes his head with a small laugh. "Don't worry, Luna. They don't scare easily." He presses a kiss to my lips, and I find myself melting a bit in his arms. The intensity of my emotions is giving me whiplash again. Although with all these men, I have to say that it's definitely more of the dicklash.

"How about the three of us—" Damian begins, but pauses when he sees Elias tense. "Or the four of us go somewhere? I think that Lars can deal with orientation, and I feel like you could use a bit of a break."

"A break? I haven't worked in my own freaking store in days," I whisper, squeezing my eyes shut. I take a deep breath and know that he's right, I need a break. If nothing else, to tell them about what I witnessed in Black Moon Magick. "Fuck, fine. Lars?" I yell to the back of the store.

"Just go," he says with a smile, shaking his head. "You'll scare the customers."

Chapter 25

Landyn

A loud buzzing pulls me from sleep, and I swipe my hand across my nightstand, trying to feel for my phone. I grab it, pushing the button on the side, and look at my messages. Five new messages show from Reggie.

Reg: Where the fuck are you?

Reg: If you don't answer the damn phone, I'm going to kick in your motherfucking door.

Reg: Neither of us is working tonight. Oakley can watch the doors.

Reg: I'm losing my fucking patience, Lan.

Reg: I warned you.

I just get to the last message when I hear a loud crash. "Are you fucking serious?" I yell, hopping out of bed and walking into my living room.

"Nice cock," Reggie says, eyebrows raised, as he pushes my partially shattered door back into place.

I snarl and turn around, walking back into my room to throw on some clothes. I pull on some dark grey sweatpants and a black tank, then go into the bathroom to throw some water on my face.

Walking back into my living room, I see Reggie sitting on the couch, relaxing like he didn't just break my fucking door. "What the fuck are you going to do about all that?" I ask through my teeth, glaring at him in annoyance.

"It can be a project for us," Reggie says with a smile. "Now take a seat. We're going to be chicks today and talk it out."

"Reg, I don't want to fucking talk shit out. I just want to get on with it," I snarl, feeling extra growly today.

Reggie clasps his hands together. "Great! So, to Beastie Besties? Or would you rather text Calluna and ask her to come here?"

"What? No. Get on with my life, forget about this shit. Move on." I sit down next to him and put my face in my hands.

"Nope, that isn't an option. You need to get over this shit. She likes you for some fucking reason, and I know it can't be your kind demeanor and charm. You're a grumpy motherfucker, and it's attractive to a limit. Now, get over the broody shit, and head out and get your girl."

"She's my mate." I whisper the words like saying them any louder will make them that much more real, and that's the last thing I need right now.

"Congrats, buddy!" he says, slapping me on my shoulder. "Even more reason to get off your ass and go get your girl."

I swing my arm, pushing his congratulations off. Standing and walking over to the wall, I slam my fist into it, cracking the plaster. "Don't you fucking understand? I'm no good for her. You of all people should fucking know. The things I've done... I fucking murdered people, Reg. Hell, I kidnapped you and Rose!" I sit back down and put my face in my hands. "It couldn't work. I'm too fucked up."

"No, what you're being is fucking ridiculous. You know that wasn't you. I don't blame you, Rose doesn't blame you, the Whitakers don't blame you! Do you think Calluna is going to give a shit about any of that? We all have pasts, and have shit we've done that we aren't proud of. If all you have is shit that you did while under the influence of a fucking psychopath, then you're a lot better than most."

"I don't deserve her," I rasp, my throat clenching.

Reg shrugs and leans farther back into the couch. "You know what, maybe you're right. If Calluna can't get over that shit, then maybe you're better off. I mean, Rose watched Finn, Dean, and Sebastian fuck different women every night for years while she loved them, never knowing that it was her they wanted. That they avoided her because of their own natures. Maybe Calluna couldn't get over it, I mean, she's no Rose."

My fists clench, and I tremble in fury. My body is up in a second, and I have Reggie by the collar of his shirt and throw him against the wall. "You don't know what the fuck you're talking about!" I yell, grinding my jaw.

"Don't I?" Reg snaps, his fangs flashing at me and his nostrils flaring. "What kind of person would reject their mate because of their own bullshit? I can only imagine how that must feel." He pushes against my shoulders, and I fly off him. I glare at him, and his shoulders tense, preparing for a fight. I stare at him in annoyance, every muscle in my body rigid in anger.

Unsure whether he is speaking of me or Calluna anymore, I shake my head and sit back down. "What am I supposed to do? I don't want to hurt her."

"Oh, I'm more than positive that you're hurting her now.

At least by the way she left last night, barely holding back tears. If you weren't one of my best fucking friends, I would have kicked your ass for treating her that way." Reggie looks at me seriously. "You're fucking this up before it even starts. You think you hate your life now? Imagine trying to fight this for the rest of your existence. What are you going to do? Leave town? How are you going to face this woman that you've crushed, all because you aren't man enough to get over your own shit? You have to forgive yourself, Landyn. We've all forgiven you, because there was *nothing* to forgive. Get out of your own fucking head and stop acting like a dick."

I sigh loudly, leaning my head back and staring up at the ceiling. "Are you going to help me fix my fucking door?"

Reggie laughs, slapping my shoulder again. "Of course, we'll fix your door and your wall. Then I'll help you remove your head out of your ass, 'cause it seems to be up there pretty far." He smiles at me, and I can't help but smile back. "After all that, you're going to take your broody ass out of this house and go find Calluna. Tell her you're sorry that you're such an asshole, and that you'll spend the rest of your life making it up to her."

"Ugh." I exhale, nodding my head. "When did you become so sensitive?"

"Always have been. I'm the total package. Hard and sexy exterior with a soft and sensitive interior." The corner of his mouth lifts into a cocky smile.

"Shut up and help me fix this door," I say, standing and pulling him in for a hug. "Thanks, man."

Chapter 26

Calluna

$\mathcal{I}$ find myself sitting at a nearby park, lying on the top of a picnic table with my arm across my head dramatically. Rhett, Damian, and Elias sit around the table, just looking at me. I can only imagine how this looks to those around us. I lean my head to the side and see a woman with gorgeous red hair, yelling out names and scanning the area as children run wildly around. I vaguely recognize her as the woman that runs the orphanage down the road—Lupine, I believe. Four very attractive men run around chasing the children, and her laughter fills the air. *Well, she makes it look easy.*

Damian clasps my hand in his, gently rubbing his thumb along my palm. Goosebumps spread over my body at his touch, and I feel myself relax a bit. "Are you okay, *mi Luna*?" he asks, and I see his brow creasing in concern when I look over at him.

"Yes, I'm fine. This is all just a bit much," I reply as I wave my hand in a circle, indicating the three of them. "Add in a fourth mate that has rejected me, and I'm feeling a little overwhelmed."

"A fourth mate who rejected you?" Rhett asks with worry.

"Landyn. He works at Vee." I sigh loudly, feeling my heart clench in pain as I think about him. "He has some… issues. I went to him last night and we had sex, then he freaked out saying that he couldn't do this." A weight suddenly settles on my heart, and my vision blurs with tears.

"Is he the one that killed all those vampires a few months ago? I read something about it online. A woman named Shani put him in a trance," Damian asks as he continues to rub small circles on my hand.

"Yeah, that's him," I say, my voice cracking. A vision of him from last night flashes in my mind, his face twisted in pain and anger.

"How could he reject you?" Elias asks in wonder, looking at me with a furrowed brow.

"I don't know. I mean, less than an hour ago, *you* were saying that I couldn't be your mate because there's darkness in me," I spit out, gritting my teeth and looking back up at the sky.

Damian and Rhett both growl at my words, and I look over to see them both glaring at Elias in anger. "What the fuck?" Rhett curses, staring daggers at Elias.

"I was just surprised. The realization that I would have to fall took me off guard." He threads a hand through his hair, and I feel the urge to push my fingers through it as well. "I am more than willing to fall for you, *mi alma*, it's just a surprise. But a happy one."

"You have to fall? From what? Grace?" I ask, my breath catching.

"Yes. I will give up my place in Heaven to fully reside

here on Earth. I am a fighter, a power angel. The time I spend here on Earth is spent fighting evil for the Makers," he admits, and I feel guilty that I'm making yet another man suffer.

"Evil, like me?" I ask quietly, knowing now why he was so aggressive at finding his mate outside of a dark magic store.

"Luna. You aren't evil," Damian says, squeezing my hand and placing his other hand on my cheek.

"You don't understand...I do practice dark magic. It began when I started finding the cursed animals, and I did it to remove the curses. It comes naturally to me as a changeling," I confess, squeezing my eyes shut. I wait as the silence engulfs me, wondering if these three will also leave. If they too will reject me.

"Okay," Damian declares resolutely, and I open my eyes to see all three men nodding.

I gape. "Okay?"

"You aren't evil, beautiful. So you practice dark magic? We all do things that are a little bad, too. We all have our demons and things we aren't proud of. We may have just met, but I know you here," Rhett says, pointing to his chest. "You have my heart, and I want you whether you're an angel or the devil herself." He leans forward, pressing his lips to mine tenderly as he supports himself above me on the picnic table. I feel as if I sink into the wood below me as he pulls my heart back to life with his gentleness.

"I'm sorry about this, you guys. All of this," I say as Rhett and I break our kiss. "I don't regret having you guys in my life, even you, Elias, with the whole caveman act. I think I know what spurred all this on, and I can't help but think that it may have never happened, and you wouldn't all be having to give up so much."

"What do you mean?" Elias asks, quirking a brow at me.

"This." I sigh as I pull the book from my bag. I hold out *Love Blooms* by C. C. Pine to the guys.

"Nice sword," Rhett says with a laugh before Damian pulls the book from his hands.

"It's spelled. I believe that when I read this book, it sparked the mate connection between us all. It explains why when I first met Landyn, or even you guys, there wasn't the instant spark, but then after reading the book, it was there. So, *I* did this," I confess, letting out a harsh breath.

"Did you spell the book?" Elias asks, scooting down the bench so that his face is closer to mine.

"No."

"Did you know it was spelled?" he asks.

"No, but maybe I should have," I groan.

"You didn't do this, Calluna, and I truly doubt the book was spelled strongly enough to create a connection out of nowhere. There had to be something there first. Mate connections don't just happen because of magic, though they can be sparked by magic, especially if there is some underlying issue that would be blocking the connection. As Rhett said, we all have our own issues. Things that would stand in the way of the connection sparking on its own. This book..." He grabs it from Damian's hands. "This book only sparked something that was already present. Even if I had seen you on the street for the first time today, without the spark, I would have found myself deeply attracted to you. Then when you began yelling at me, I would have been just as lost as I am now. No one yells at a power angel. We generate fear in those around us, not aggression. You were screaming and growling at me in the middle of the street. You did not bend to my commands. You got moody and stomped away like a petulant child." He chuckles, putting his fingers against my cheek and touching me for the first time. His touch causes heat to course through my veins and my heart to skitter. I stare into his flecked copper eyes, the compulsion to kiss him making my breath catch.

"I'm not a petulant child," I say the words breathily, unable to generate any anger behind them.

"You kind of were." He chuckles, tapping me on the nose. His large hand holds my face in place, and he looks at me as if battling himself. His fingertips push slightly into the back of my head as he pulls my face towards his and allows our lips to connect for the first time. Desire radiates between us as heat pools in my belly. Without breaking our kiss, he stands and pulls me into a sitting position, then I wrap my legs around him. His hands drag down my back until they reach my ass, which he cups to hold me in place.

"Piny! Look at them, they're kissing!" a little girl squeals to Lupine, causing Elias and me to break apart quickly. I laugh and loosen the hold my legs have on him.

"Give me a second," Elias says breathlessly. "I'd rather the little girl not see how much I enjoyed that kiss."

"Same," Damian and Rhett say at the same time, making me laugh louder, and my chest already feels so much lighter.

Chapter 27

Calluna

After being caught making out by a small child, we decide to leave the park and head to my apartment. I ask them to come with me, not only because I want to rip their fucking clothes off and don't want to get arrested for public indecency, but also because I need to talk to them about the shit I saw at Black Moon Magick. Fear radiates through me at the memory of the power I witnessed from the two brothers as they stood over the corpse of the bird.

I unlock the door to my apartment and invite the guys in, pointing to the couch and telling them to sit down while I go into the kitchen to get drinks. I walk out with beers, handing one to each of the men and sitting down in the space between Damian and Rhett. Jake runs into the room and leaps onto Elias' lap, causing him to jump and almost spill his beer.

"What the hell? You have a monkey?" he asks, eyes wide.

"Yup, that's Jake," I say, then make a kissing noise to call him to me. He runs across Damian's legs and onto my lap, purring and meowing as I rub his tiny head.

"Why is he meowing?" Elias asks, still looking completely stunned that not only do I have a monkey in my apartment, but that it meows.

"He has a species disorder. He cycles through different animals from time to time. Don't you, baby boy?" I coo to Jake. "This is one of the reasons I asked you guys to come to my apartment."

"You wanted to show us your monkey?" Rhett questions with a wink and a flirty smile.

I clench my thighs together, wanting nothing more than to show them my metaphorical monkey. Refraining from doing just that, I shake my head with a small smile. "No. Jake was one of the cursed animals that I came across. There was a darkness in him, much like the darkness I saw in you, Rhett, the night Damian brought you into my shop. The same black smoke you described seeing that night was always present in the creatures brought in. There have been several animals found like this, but the police force doesn't seem to take them very seriously. I began practicing dark magic as a way to remove the curses. Although, as I had very little knowledge of the way the magic worked, and no one to really mentor me, I was only able to remove a bit of the bad magic. There are always traces left behind. Quirks that make them different than a normal animal."

"Do I have any traces?" Rhett asks.

"I don't think so. The animal that I uncursed before you was Klaus, and the only trace left on him is his rash issue. I think you're the first time I was completely successful. I used my blood and Damian's. That may have been the key."

"Who is doing this?" Elias asks, addressing the three of

us, since we've been directly involved in the incidents. "Did you two see anything?"

"Not really," Damian says, shaking his head.

"I went to Black Moon Magick today to speak with the owner, Falcar, about the book. When I went in, I saw him and his brother doing magic over a dead bird." Anxiety knots my stomach as I think of what I saw today and the fear I felt when Nelcar pinned me against the wall as if I was nothing. "They caught me, and one of the brothers, Nelcar, attacked me. He held me in place with magic until Falcar told him to let me go."

Elias' hand clenches, and a snarl leaves his lips. "He hurt you?"

I nod, biting my lip. "They're dangerous. I don't know what we can do, but we have to do something."

Damian and Rhett both put their hands on my thighs comfortingly, giving them a small squeeze. "We'll figure something out," Damian breathes. "We should go to the police."

"What will the police do if they haven't done anything so far?" Rhett asks. "We should go down there and sort this out ourselves."

"Rhett, we aren't fucking superheroes. Luna is the only one that knows magic. Don't be rash," Damian snaps.

"Did you say rash? Where?" Rhett shouts, looking around his body and pulling a laugh from me.

"How about this, we call the police station and give them our account of the night Rhett was attacked, and then Luna can tell them more about the animals she has brought into the shop. Give them our suspicions of the brothers at Black Moon Magick, and hope that they do their jobs," Damian offers rationally.

"Okay…" I say, knowing this is the safest plan of action.

There's no way I could take on the brothers alone. I have no grasp on my powers at all. Hell, even the black sparks I experienced today with Elias are new to me, and I have no idea if I could even replicate the action.

Damian calls the Silver Springs Police Department and gives an officer his full account of what's been happening, then he passes the phone to Rhett and me to fill in the rest. The officer says that he'll look into it and question the brothers at Black Moon Magick, but as it isn't illegal to practice dark magic, there isn't much they can do without concrete proof. I feel dejected, but hope they can uncover something that will end this.

I flip on the television, and the four of us start watching some movie that Rhett picked when Elias gets up.

"I have to go, *mi alma*. There is still some angel business I have to take care of, but I will come back." He pulls me up from the couch and into his arms. The transition from the caveman I met earlier today to this sweet man holding me is like night and day. His strong arms hold me against his chest, and I melt a bit as he bends his face down to press his lips to mine, dragging his tongue against my lips until I allow him entry. He explores me slowly before releasing me, pressing a last kiss to my forehead before he walks out the door. I return to the couch, feeling two small holes in my heart from his and Landyn's absences.

Chapter 28

Damian

Calluna sits between Rhett and me, leaning her head on my shoulder and placing her hand on my leg. Her touch electrifies me to my bones. I've known this woman for just a few short days, and already I feel how deeply she has burrowed herself into my heart. Evil? Not a chance. There isn't one part of me that could ever believe that this beautiful woman was evil. The amount of love she shows for the animals around her, keeping all these 'broken' animals, is nothing but pure goodness. She may have darkness in her, but like Rhett said, we all do. Does her darkness overshadow her light, though? No.

I watch as Rhett's hand rests on her thigh, much higher than before, and I know that he's struggling to hold himself together. The need to have her pushes on both of us. When she and Elias shared their first kiss in the park, the passion that ignited between them had me hard as a rock, wishing I was the one at her lips. Everything about her calls to me. Her soft pouty lips, her beautiful caramel skin, her blue-green eyes. The tank top she has on barely covers her large, supple breasts, and I want nothing more than to feel them in my palms. To run my lips against her hardened nipples.

I shift on the couch, trying to adjust the bulge in my pants, and my movement causes her to look at me. She takes in my heavy-lidded gaze with her lips slightly parted and her breaths quickening. Unable to hold back, I bend forward and press my lips to hers, kissing her gently, asking her permission to go further. I don't want to push her, or to rush this situation that already must have her feeling as if her world has been flipped upside down. The hand she had resting on my leg begins to climb higher as she deepens our kiss, opening her mouth for me. The small inch she gives me causes me to snap, and I lean into her, making love to her mouth. Her hand stops sliding up my leg when she reaches her destination, and she cups the bulge in my jeans, making my cock twitch in her grasp.

She shifts further into me, and our kiss breaks as her tank top is pulled over her head. My eyes connect with Rhett's, and I see the same fire burning in his as I feel burning in mine. He tosses her shirt to the floor, making fast work of the clasp on the back of her bra and pulling that off as well. Once her breasts are free, I lean forward to drag my tongue against the dark tips, causing her breaths to quicken. I feel Rhett's hands dragging down her stomach, then one comes up to grasp at the breast opposite of the one I'm licking and sucking. She moans as he pinches her other nipple and places kisses and bites along her neck.

"Where is your bedroom, beautiful?" Rhett asks in her ear, using that husky voice of his that makes me completely wild.

"Through the kitchen," she moans, moving to stand. I grab onto her waist and stand, pulling her close to me. She wraps her legs around my waist as I carry her in the direction she pointed, allowing Rhett to lead the way. He opens a door, revealing a small bedroom with a king-sized bed. Calluna turns, and we watch as Rhett strips, pulling his shirt off and throwing it to the ground. Then he pushes down his jeans and boxers at the same time, displaying how hard he is. No matter how many times I see this man's body, I still find myself as rigid as the first time. He's a thing of beauty with his tanned skin and his hard-muscled chest. His abs are so fucking lickable that I feel the urge to drag my tongue against them right now. His cock is thick and long, the sight causing me to groan as I recall how amazing it feels as he pushes inside me. Calluna turns to me and takes in my turned-on state, gazing at me hungrily.

"I want to see you together," she purrs, and my cock jerks in my pants.

"Are you sure? We're more than happy to concentrate on you," I whisper to her, while finding myself deeply turned on at her eagerness to watch us together.

"I'm sure," she replies, her gaze heated.

I lay her on the bed, then bend over to pull her leggings from her body, dragging my tongue against her skin on the way down. I grasp her ankles and tug her body towards me, pulling her ass to the edge of the bed. I kneel down with my knees on the floor and stare at her pussy, dripping with need for the two of us. Unable to resist any longer, I lean forward and spread her for me, then drag my tongue against her slit, stopping to swirl around her clit. She jerks on the bed as I continue to feast on her, and I look up to see Rhett kissing her lips, then moving to capture her nipples in his mouth. We continue to push her into a frenzy, and her thighs quiver as she holds my head in place. Pleas fall from her lips, and I groan as my cock presses hard against my jeans, aching to be touched. I push two of my fingers inside her and slide them in and out easily with her juices, feeling her clench around them as she's pushed closer and closer to the edge while I nibble and suck on her greedy clit.

"I'm coming!" she screams as her core tightens around my fingers, causing my cock to ache, wishing I was inside her as she comes. *Soon enough.*

She lies on the edge of the bed, her body now slack, and Rhett pulls her towards him and sits her up at the head of the bed. Watching him kiss her passionately, I begin removing my jeans and allow them to pool at my feet as I begin stroking myself. Rhett crawls towards me on his knees and pulls me onto the bed with him, grasping the back of my neck roughly and crashing his mouth into mine. I moan against his lips as he kisses me, panting as our stiff cocks rub against each other. I reach down and grip his shaft, using the pre-cum to glide my hand up and down with ease.

Rhett bites back a moan and pushes me back so that I'm lying beside Luna, then he crawls between us, moving from her lips to mine while always keeping a hand on the other person. He strokes my cock as he kisses her lips and drags his fingers along her slit as he kisses mine, driving us both into a frenzy. Unable to take much more, I grasp the back of his head, giving a gentle push down to where I want him. He accepts his new position with eagerness, dragging his tongue against the bottom of my cock and then pulling the entire shaft in his mouth. I buck my hips upward, encouraging him to take more of me, and curse as I hit the back of his throat, which he clenches around the sensitive head. I bite my lip and look over to Luna as she stares in wonder while he sucks my cock in earnest, his moans vibrating down my shaft and causing me to grit my teeth. I watch in anticipation as Luna crawls down my side and finds a position next to Rhett, getting a closer look as he works me over. Her soft fingers reach out and cup my balls, causing me to twitch in his mouth, and it takes everything in me to not come. She takes in my reaction with a smile, that dark side she spoke about earlier coming to the surface.

"Let's torture him a bit, beautiful," Rhett growls, then he drags his lips and teeth along the side of my cock as she does the same, a husky moan leaving her lips. They continue their ministrations, working me into a frenzy. I'm barely holding it together, unsure of whether to beg them to stop or to beg them to let me come. Wanting to be inside her, I go with the former and pull Luna up my chest, kissing her passionately. Rhett follows suit, pressing a kiss to her lips, then one to mine, finding a way to touch us both.

"I need inside you, *mi Luna*. Do you think you can take us both?" I ask, my voice barely a rasp.

"Yes, please," she begs, crawling on top of me and lining her core up to my aching cock. Her wetness already has me twitching, and I grit my teeth to hold myself together, knowing that I won't last long. She grasps me at the base and slowly impales herself on me, soft moans leaving her lips as she slides down inch by inch. The sight of my cock slowly disappearing into her heat is the hottest fucking thing I've ever witnessed, and I lock eyes with Rhett, begging him to take her too.

"Do you have lube, beautiful?" he asks, coming up behind her and pushing her hair to one side to give him access to lick and suck on her neck.

"Yes," she moans as she slides up and down on my cock. "Nightstand drawer."

Rhett leans over and grabs the tube, squirting a generous amount onto his cock and then against her back entrance. "Have you done this before, beautiful?" he asks, barely hiding the intensity of his question. I too await her answer, as I'm unhappy at the idea of any men other than her four mates touching her. Fuck, I won't even be pleased with Landyn touching her until he begs for forgiveness after hurting her.

"No," she says breathily, her blue-green eyes locking with mine. "Anal sex never interested me until now."

A sigh of satisfaction leaves both Rhett's and my lips, and I know we're fucking dicks for being pleased about this. But shifters take pride in claiming every inch of their mates, and the fact that no man has entered her there has me once again trying my hardest to hold my shit together.

"Relax," I tell her as I rub her thighs which are squeezing me tightly, trying to comfort her. I feel as Rhett begins to push into her and continue to rub her legs to help her stay calm as he enters her and a wince crosses her lips. I groan when she's fully seated on both of our cocks, feeling Rhett's cock against my own through her thin wall. We both begin to move, sawing in and out of her, our moans all mixing as we work each other closer and closer to release.

Sliding my hand between us, I begin to circle her clit with my thumb. She shudders, soft sighs leaving her lips as she begins to beg us to go faster. I thrust up into her, panting as I impale her on my cock, and her nails dig into my chest. I feel her legs begin to quiver as her core clenches, milking me and permitting me to explode. I continue to slam into her, picking up my pace as the base of my spine tingles and cum shoots out of me in jets. Her orgasm pulls Rhett over the edge, and he grabs her breasts tightly in his hands as he slams into her once more, filling her ass with ropes of his own thick cum.

They both collapse on top of me, and breathy laughs leave all our lips as our cocks begin to soften and fall from her body. Rhett moves off the bed and into the adjoining bathroom, allowing Luna to roll over to my side, her head nestled on my arm. I place kisses on the top of her head and enjoy the feel of her fingers gently caressing my chest. Rhett appears with two warm, wet rags and begins to clean her pussy and ass, tossing the second one to me to clean myself up. My heart melts as I watch him clean her, then he moves to place a kiss on her lips before putting both rags in the dirty laundry and cuddling into her other side with his arm around us both.

"I love you both," she says softly, hiding her face in my chest. "I know it's too soon, but I do. Thank you for giving me one of the best nights of my life."

"I love you too, *mi Luna. Tuyo para siempre*," I whisper into her hair.

"I love you too, beautiful girl. Forever and always," Rhett says, placing a kiss onto the back of her neck. We spend the rest of the night entangled with each other until we all fall asleep.

Chapter 29

Calluna

I wake up early to a soft knocking on my front door. I sit up and look at the two naked men asleep beside me, and I'm unable to stop the smile from crossing my lips. These two men, who fucked me into oblivion last night, have officially claimed my heart, and I feel lighter than I have felt in years. I crawl from the bed gently, so I don't disturb the guys, and walk over to pull on some shorts and throw on a t-shirt, not bothering with a bra or panties. I grab a hair-tie from my dresser and pull my hair up as I walk to the front door, then open it slowly to see whoever has decided to wake me this early on this blissful day.

My jaw drops when I see the one man I never expected to see, standing at my door and looking down at me warily. "Lars gave me your address last night, but he told me to come over in the morning. That you were a morning person?" Landyn says uneasily, looking me over as if realizing that the statement wasn't true.

"Lars is an asshole," I say with a scowl, then I open the door fully and walk to my couch, allowing him to decide whether he will be staying or going. I look at him with my brows raised. "Did you at least bring coffee?"

"No, I didn't," he says, his brows knitted. His eyes have a haunted look as he slowly shuts the door and walks over to the couch. He sits next to me, but leaves enough space so that another person could sit between us. "I came to apologize for the way I acted."

"Oh?" I ask, my tone snarky. I don't feel like letting him off the hook that easily.

"Yes. I was an asshole. I am an asshole." He sighs loudly. "But I don't want to be an asshole to you. I meant what I said, I'm no good for you."

"Landyn, if you came over here to rehash why you're rejecting me as your mate, save it. I don't need to hear it again. Just go ahead and sever the tie, then we can both go our separate ways." Sadness tears at my chest as I say the words, but I mean them. I won't allow him to toy with my emotions. Not when I have two men in the other room that are willing to give themselves over to me fully and another that has said he's willing to actually fall for me.

A sob catches in my throat as I avoid his eyes. "I won't be toyed with, Landyn. I don't blame you for the hurt that you suffer. You've been through a lot, and your pain is justified. I won't deny that I want you and that this hurts more than I ever believed possible, but if you're unwilling to give us a chance, then just please go. I set you free of the ropes that bind you to me."

He closes the space between us in a flash, his chestnut brown eyes locked with mine. "I can't be without you, Callie. I know that I'm no good for you, but I'm selfish enough to say fuck it. I have a lot of shit, a lot of it, and I'm going to be a complete asshole sometimes. I'm going to drive you fucking nuts. My moods are explosive, and I sometimes hide behind my silent demeanor. I just ask that you give me another chance. I don't deserve it, but I'm still asking for it. I promise you, Callie, that I will spend every day of the rest of my life trying to make this up to you. To be worthy of you."

My eyes well with tears as I listen to him pour his heart out to me, his breath shaking as he begs me to forgive him. His hand moves to my cheek, wiping away a tear before pulling his lips to mine. He kisses me hard, like he needs me as much as he needs air to breathe. I sob against his lips as he pulls me onto his lap, his fingers wrapped in my hair.

"Say you'll forgive me, Callie. Please?" he says between kisses, clutching at me like he's afraid I'll escape him. I pull away from him and look into those beautiful eyes that seem to be shining in fear, feeling his heart drumming in his chest below my palm.

"Yes," I sob, pulling his lips back to mine. "I forgive you." He lays his forehead against mine, just holding me to him. I turn so that I lie in his arms on the couch and slowly fall back asleep. His tight grasp on me never loosens.

"Well, isn't this a sweet sight?"

The sound of voices pulls me from sleep, and I shift slightly, recognizing that I'm still on the couch. Landyn's arms tighten around me, and I look up at him to see that he too fell asleep. Rhett stands in the doorway between my kitchen and living room, watching us on the couch with a smile on his face.

Damian walks up behind him, his eyes zeroing in on Landyn, and he frowns. "You must be Landyn."

I sit up, stretching and yawning loudly, and feel Landyn's hand still sitting on my side as I move. "I am," Landyn says, his voice thick with sleep.

"Think you'll stick around this time?" Damian asks, the frown still on his face.

"Damian," I say stiffly, surprised to see him being so aggressive. Landyn's body stiffens behind me, but he nods his head.

"As long as she'll have me. I have a lot of ground to make up," he says seriously, looking at Damian.

"I'm glad you recognize that," Damian says as he walks up to where we're sitting on the couch. He puts his hand out, his face looking less severe but still lacking the warmth I'm used to. "I'm Damian."

Landyn reaches up and shakes his hand, his other hand never leaving my side. Rhett walks in behind Damian and also offers his hand, a smile on his face. "I'm Rhett. Glad to see you, dude."

I shake my head, biting my lip and relaxing slightly.

"Have you heard from Elias at all?" Rhett asks, sitting down next to me on the couch and pulling my legs into his lap.

I frown, looking around for my phone. "No, I haven't. I don't even have his number."

Damian exits the room and returns, handing me my phone and sitting on the other side of Rhett, then he places a kiss on the man's lips. "He put it in there when we were at the park."

I slide my thumb against the screen and move to my contacts, scanning through the names for Elias, but seeing nothing. I continue to scroll until I see a new entry named 'Fallen Dick,' and I smile to myself as I click the entry and type out a quick message. Almost no time passes before I have a reply.

Me: Good morning, Azrael.

Fallen Dick: Good morning, *mi alma*. I will be there soon.

Chapter 30

Elias

Leaving *mi alma*'s apartment last night was one of the hardest things that I've ever had to do. Now that I've found her, I don't want to be without her. *Ever.* Even if that means falling from grace, so that I will never be called away from her. Power angels are required to fight evil for the Makers, meaning that I could be called away at any time, which makes settling pretty much impossible. Most power angels find no reason to settle, as most of us do not have mates. Falling isn't something an angel aspires to do, not *good* ones at least. But for Calluna, I would give it all up.

The biggest thing I need to figure out is how to fall but still keep my wings, as I have become very attached to them. This has led me to search for one of the demons I would normally have been sent to kill. Our paths have crossed before, but I always spared him because I never felt he committed any truly evil acts, just that he had fallen. My biggest reason for trying to talk to him is that he found a way to keep his wings.

I walk through the dark wooded area in a forest just outside of Borneo. I can sense his presence, but for whatever reason, he has kept himself hidden. I look through the trees, trying to discern the shapes around me. Flashes of gunmetal gray feathers appear in my peripheral vision, and I decide to sit on a nearby fallen log, attempting to show that I didn't come here for a confrontation.

"Alaric, I mean you no harm," I say loudly, my voice echoing in the forest.

"Empty words coming from a power such as yourself." A deep voice emits from a copse of trees to my right, and I look over in time to see a man emerge from the darkness. He's built so broadly, his shadow seems to cast out as far as the eye can see. His large gunmetal gray wings spread out behind him and his shaggy black hair falls to cover one of his eyes, but his corded muscles are tense. "What do you want from me, Elias? I have done nothing to warrant this visit."

"I come to you not as a power, but as an angel looking to fall," I say, forcing as much truth into the words as possible.

He quirks a brow at me, pushing his long, black hair from his face. "Why would you want to fall?" he asks me skeptically, his muscles rippling as he steps closer to me.

"My reasons are my own. You fell, and I asked not what made you make the choice. If I wanted to kill you, I could have done it many times over, but I have always spared you. I am only here because you have kept your wings, and that is what *I* want."

Alaric laughs, a cold smile crossing his lips. "*Spared me.*" He rolls his eyes as he continues to walk toward me, until he stands in front of me, a towering wall of a man. "A woman," he says condescendingly.

"Excuse me?" I ask, standing in front of him menacingly, but I still have to look up to meet his eyes.

"I fell from grace for a woman. A kitsune." He smiles, looking behind him. I follow his gaze and watch as a thin woman with long, charcoal gray hair framing her face emerges from the copse of trees. She is petite, but stands with a fierceness that shows she is one to be reckoned with. She bares her teeth at me in a ruthless smile, and my eyes widen slightly as I look back to Alaric. "Three strikes, that is all we get before we fall. Each strike shrinks our wings until, *poof*. They are gone."

"But you found a way to keep yours," I insist, looking at the large appendages in question.

"Yes. Normally the fall is a slow thing. Each strike happens one by one as we slowly lose the innate *goodness* that we were created with. Not many want to fall, so they struggle to repress the sins that would lead to it. When I met her, though—" He pauses as she approaches him, moving to place herself against his side. She fits there perfectly, as if she is the missing piece to his puzzle, and his large body encases her beside him. "I met Aishah and found that I no longer needed grace. I needed her with every piece of my being. *Qing ren.*"

She looks up at him, murmuring the words of her native language to him. The look she gives him is enough to make even my heart ache. "*Qinaide.*"

He bends to place a gentle kiss on her lips, then his eyes move back to me. "Commit the three strikes at once, three sins that would lead to your fall. That is how I retained my wings."

I nod, knowing what I must do to keep *mi cielo*. I put my hand out, clasping Alaric's shoulder in a show of brotherhood. "Thank you, my brother. I am glad that you found peace."

He reaches up and clasps my shoulder in return, a knowing smile on his face. "For it is for them. They are the reason that we all would fall. Over and over again." He looks down at his Aishah, who smiles at him like he is the light of her life. The light of a fallen angel, I think with a laugh. I nod to her in thanks and turn, moving into a run as I fly out of the forest and back to my Calluna.

I come back to Silver Springs and walk into the small apartment I have been renting during my time here. I keep very few belongings there, so packing them up takes no time at all. I am still unsure what my three consecutive sins will be, but I hope that they will come to me in time. My phone vibrates in my pocket, and I look down to see a message come in.

Mi Alma: Good morning, Azrael.

I chuckle at her use of yet another angel's name that isn't my own, joy warming in my heart that I am lucky enough to have found her. *Mi cielo*, my heaven.

Me: Good morning, *mi alma*. I will be there soon.

I slip my phone back into my pocket and grab my bag, throwing it over my shoulder. It is abrupt, but hopefully Calluna will be okay with me moving in. Because that is exactly what I'm doing. I refuse to spend another minute without her, for she is mine for all eternity.

Flying to her apartment building takes me no time at all, and I am up to her floor in a flash, my hand positioned to knock on the door, when I hear voices inside. The voices of Rhett and Damian I recognize, but the third male is unknown to my ears, and I am unable to stop myself from bursting through the door without invitation. Calluna's eyes widen as I enter the room, my bag dropping to the floor with a loud thump. Damian, Rhett, and the third man stand quickly at my hasty entrance, and only Damian and Rhett relax when they see who I am. The third man eyes me with his teeth clenched and his lips drawing back in a snarl.

"Who is this?" I growl, moving quickly into the man's face. I can only assume this is Landyn, the fourth mate that rejected her, that hurt *mi alma*.

Calluna stands, putting a hand on my chest. "Elias, it's okay. This is Landyn," she says cautiously.

"Right," I growl, my fist moving of its own accord as I slam it into the man's face. Rhett moves in a flash, using his fox speed to snatch Calluna out of the way as Landyn retaliates. His hand partially shifts, turning into long talons that he drags across my chest as his own wings emerge from his back. A nearby lamp flies to the floor, the glass shattering as it is knocked down by the large expanse of our wings as we attack each other without care. I throw him without preamble, and his body crumples into the wall as I stand above him. "*You* are the one that has forsaken my mate, that crushed her beautiful soul. *Cómo te atreves?*"

"Elias!" Calluna yells as she pulls herself out of Rhett's arms and gets into my face. My eyes flash in anger as I feel the first sin settle on my soul, *wrath*. My hand comes out and grabs her by the back of her neck, my fingers lacing in her hair as I pull her into my arms, settling her core against me.

"*Te quiero. Te necesito*," I growl to her in Spanish as *lust* overwhelms my senses. "I want you, *mi amor*. I *need* you." Her blue-green eyes blaze, and her breathing becomes hitched as her desire for me flickers in her eyes. The fingers on my other hand lightly graze along her cheek, moving down her neck, then moving to the collar of her shirt. In one swift motion, I rip the cloth from her body, watching as it falls to the floor. My cock hardens as I see that she is wearing nothing beneath the now destroyed article of clothing. I connect my eyes with hers, willing her to give me the permission to take her as lust pulsates through me. Her pupils dilate, and she gives a slow nod of her head as she bites her lip and I break.

My right hand clenches in her hair, pulling her head back and giving me better access to her throat, where I pepper her with rough kisses. I drag my teeth down until I reach her full breasts, and I take one of her peaks into my mouth, swirling my tongue around the nub and pulling away with it between my teeth. She hisses out, thrusting against me and making my cock twitch. I throw her onto the couch behind us and bend down to pull her small shorts from her body, reveling in the sight of her pussy, when I realize she wore no undergarments under her clothing. I drag my tongue against her, relishing her sweet taste on my tongue as she writhes under my mouth. I draw her higher, wanting her wet and ready for me when I finally plunge into her, when I take her for the first time and fall from grace. Her nails dig into my shoulders as I suck and nibble on her greedy clit, moving to swipe my tongue at her entrance and drinking all of her essence, unwilling to waste a single drop.

Feeling her quiver, I reach down and unbutton my pants, releasing my cock. Wrapping my fingers around its thickness, I begin pumping, feeling it twitch with need in my grasp. "*Te amo, mi cielo*," I growl as I pull myself up against her body, leveling myself at her core. "I love you."

Her eyes widen at my words, and I choose that moment to plunge into her, falling into my own heaven. "I choose her," I growl the words out, looking heavenward. "*Renuncio a mi posición al lado de Dios. Y la elijo a ella.*"

I renounce my position at the side of God. And I choose her.

The *prideful* words leave my lips as immense pain and pleasure roar through my body. Calluna screams beneath me, her pleasure echoing within the room as her core clenches at my cock. My wings spread out and feel as if they are being ripped from my body as I shout out my own release. My eyes flash black, and I throw my head back, feeling what can only be my soul cracking within me. I look down to *mi alma* and her eyes fill with blackness as her changeling form flashes beneath me.

Chapter 31

Calluna

Coming on the cock of a falling angel... *Fuck*, that shit can make a girl *ad-dick-ted*. When Elias busted in here and his eyes landed on Landyn, I wasn't sure if he wouldn't kill the man. An unearthly rage flashed through him, so much so that it was almost palpable. I could feel his anger at the man he believed had forsaken me. I couldn't help but clench my thighs as he spit out Spanish words. His eyes locked with mine, and the desire I saw there made my whole body weaken. His words felt as if they spoke to my very soul, cracking down every defense that I had.

Te quiero, mi alma. Te necesito. I want you, mi alma. I need you.

Taken in such a way, so abruptly and in front of an audience, would've probably made me bristle and blush before I met all these men. What just happened, though, was almost instinctual. His desire called to my own, the mate connection riding me to take him. To make him mine.

"You've fallen for me?" I ask as I look up to him, my

words sounding weak as they leave my chest. My breaths come out in pants, and my throat feels tight as I take in what he has given up for me. *Everything.*

"I would fall for you over and over. You are *mine*. I love you, *mi alma*."

His soul.

Well, I'm fucking sprung. I look around the room, now having claimed all four of my mates, and I feel an odd sense of completeness. Like that uncontrollable pull is no longer there. Instead, there's a feeling of calm. Tears well in my eyes, and I quickly try to blink them away, unwilling to start crying again. As someone who typically never cries, I've been crying way more than what is acceptable lately.

"Our souls have bonded. Those are the emotions you are feeling. I give you everything I have, everything I am. We are now one. Darkness meets darkness." He says the words softly, and I see that his own eyes are shining. Uncontrollable sobs wrack my body, as if this large man's emotions give my own body permission to cry. To soak in the overwhelming feelings of what he has done for me. What I have gained in each of these men.

"Momma didn't raise no weak bitch," I sob with a small chuckle, making all the men throw their heads back in laughter as I attempt to wipe away all evidence of my emotions.

Elias presses a soft kiss to my lips, which feel bruised from our passionate kisses just moments ago. He stands and faces Landyn, his hand extended. "Are you back for good?" he asks, eyeing Landyn thoughtfully.

"Yes. I won't be leaving her again," Landyn says stiffly, looking Elias up and down with squinted eyes. I don't know if Elias being butt ass naked with my cum on his massive cock does anything to help the situation, but Landyn puts his hand out, accepting Elias'. They shake each other's hands forcefully, then release them as they continue to eye each other.

"Not that all this alpha male shit isn't hot as fuck, but you seem to be covered in two days of cum, beautiful. How about a shower?" Rhett breaks the silence, coming over to me and kneeling next to where I lie on the couch. I smile, feeling a small amount of weirdness at the fact that I've fucked three of the four men in the room in the last eight hours. This is most *definitely* not what Lars meant about getting out more.

I allow Rhett to pull me up from the couch and follow him into my bathroom, standing by the sink as he pulls back the shower curtain and turns the water on. I look at myself in the mirror and see that my hair is in a mess on my head, what little makeup I was wearing is smeared across my face, certain areas of my skin are covered in what can only be called *love bites,* and I look—for lack of a better term—well fucked.

I watch as Rhett peels off the sweatpants that hung low on his hips, showing me the rest of his gorgeous body. He puts his hand in the water, testing its temperature, before he steps in and pulls me in with him. Once we get into the water, I lean my head back, allowing the warmth to relax my muscles. Rhett takes a cup from the tub's edge and begins pouring water into my hair, then he flips the cap on my shampoo and rubs some onto my scalp. I moan as he massages the shampoo through my hair, taking great care with me. I've never been taken care of like this, and I melt into his embrace. He rinses the suds from my hair, wetting a washrag I didn't see him grab and lathering soap onto my body. He washes every part of me, and the motions make my heart clench as he touches my most intimate areas in a non-sexual way.

He makes quick work of cleaning himself while I stand in the stream of hot water, taking in every inch of his hard muscle and marveling in how stupidly pretty he is. He catches me staring and just smiles at me devilishly with a quick wink. He steps out of the shower and grabs three towels, wrapping one around his waist and handing me another to put in my hair. The last one he wraps around me as he pulls me into his chest, pressing soft kisses to my neck and shoulders.

"You are unbelievably sweet," I whisper softly. "I've never had someone take care of me like this before."

His lips freeze on my shoulder, his eyes connecting with mine in the mirror in front of us. "You deserve all this and more, beautiful. There will be no more moments where you aren't being cared for the way you deserve. You'll always have our attention, respect, loyalty, and love."

I turn in his arms and press my lips to his, sinking into his kiss. "I love you, Rhett."

"Always, beautiful girl. Always."

Chapter 32

Calluna

After my moment with Rhett in the shower, I know that I need to go check on the shop, see how the new employees are doing, and give Lars a much-needed break. He has been a lot more understanding about all this than most others would be in this situation. I walk back into the living room, now fully dressed with my blow-dried hair up in a messy bun. I look around the room to see it's in much better shape than I left it, missing the remains of the fighting and fucking that just took place. Elias looks at me sheepishly from the couch, now dressed in dark blue jeans with no shirt, his large black wings tight behind him.

He stands and walks over to me, pulling me to his chest. "Did I hurt you, Calluna?" he asks with concern furrowing his brow.

"Not at all. I feel amazing," I tell him truthfully, rolling my loose shoulders. "I do have to go to my shop though. I've been the absentee owner far too much lately. It isn't fair to Lars."

I watch as the men all nod and begin pulling on socks and shoes. "You don't have to all come with me. I mean, it's probably going to be boring. You could all just hang out here, or do whatever you normally do with your free time."

"Of course, we will accompany you," Elias states, as if the latter is the most absurd thing he has ever heard.

"Yes, I want to come," Landyn says, pulling me from Elias' arms. "Besides, I can be helpful. Step one in winning you back."

"You don't have to win me back," I tell him seriously, rolling my eyes. "I told you I forgave you."

"Let him suffer a bit, *mi Luna*," Damian says as he comes up behind me and kisses my neck. "He should win your trust back." I shiver a bit in their arms, listening to the vengeful side of Damian that I didn't know existed.

"Fine. You're cleaning out the bird cages. They're the worst," I say with a smile, tapping Landyn on the nose. He laughs deeply as he pulls me in to kiss me passionately. Jeez, all these men and all this kissing is making me want to hole up in my apartment and let them ravish me for a week or so. Heat pools between my thighs at the thought, but I shake my head, knowing that I need to adult right now.

I slip into my flats and grab my bag, then walk out the door, listening as all four men follow me. I can only imagine what the neighbors would think if they saw, until I remember that I've recently seen both Violet and Juniper with harems of their own. If it weren't for the book, I would seriously think it was something in the water.

Landyn indicates that he parked in the parking garage this morning and we can take his SUV to the shop, and I eagerly agree, since I don't have a car of my own. With my shop in walking distance and Uber available for going farther distances, I haven't seen the point in the extra expense. Especially with everything being available for delivery these days. Today, though, after all the fucking that I've been doing, I'm thankful for a ride.

"Can I drive?" I ask, hopping a bit in excitement. I haven't driven in so long, I kind of wanna get back behind the wheel, although I don't want them to know that.

"It's really big, and you're really small," Landyn says uneasily.

I frown at him, squinting my eyes menacingly. "I think it's clear from the past few days that I'm more than able to take something big, no matter how small I am. And I'm not small, you're all just freakishly tall. I'm average height." When Landyn doesn't seem like he's going to bend to my will, I stomp my foot and glare at him. "See this as step one of winning me back," I say petulantly.

"Fine, fine," Landyn agrees with a laugh, throwing me the keys. "Just be careful."

I squeal a bit and run over to the huge, black SUV, trying to use the door to pull myself in unsuccessfully. Landyn laughs loudly and grabs a hold of my ass, pushing me up into the large vehicle. "I'm going to have to install a running board and a handle, aren't I?"

"Only if you don't want to have to shove my ass in each time," I say, settling into the soft leather and adjusting the seat.

"Well then, maybe I won't," I hear him say quietly as he walks around the vehicle to get in the passenger seat. Elias, Rhett, and Damian pile into the back, and I feel thankful that the vehicle is so large, with two rows of seating in the back. I shift it into reverse and pull out far too fast, slamming on the brake and causing us all to be thrown forward.

"Everyone got your seatbelts on?" I ask with a smile, as if I did that on purpose, and start laughing hard when I see all the men quickly grabbing the belts and pulling them across their chests.

"Please don't crash my truck," Landyn says with a cautious smile, his hand holding on to the *oh-shit* handle above his head.

"Oh, we'll be fine," I say, patting the dashboard and pulling out of the garage.

When we get to Beastie Besties, we're greeted by three teens sitting outside on the curb, looking at us in confusion. I stop the SUV and hop out, the force of the ground hurting the soles of my feet a bit. Okay, maybe a running board would be good. Or at least a small step.

"What are you guys doing out here?" I ask, looking into the windows of the store to see that it's dark inside. "Is Lars not here?"

The blonde girl stands, brushing off her jeans. "He never showed up, so we've just been waiting around."

"I'm sorry." I look around, finding it *very* odd that Lars never showed up. "That is so unlike him. I hope you haven't been waiting long."

"No worries!" the girl says with a big smile.

I open the door to the store and flip on the lights, greeted by the noises of all the animals in their cages. Everyone follows in behind me, and I turn to look at my new employees again. "I'm sorry again that you guys had to wait this morning. I'm even more sorry for how you saw me acting yesterday. Life has been," I turn and look at my four guys, "a bit chaotic the past few days. Now, what are your names, and what did Lars go over with you all yesterday?"

They introduce themselves to me. The blonde girl is Beth, and the two guys with her are Dakota and Rob. There's a third guy that I saw yesterday, Logan, but the others say that he has basketball practice today. Damian told me yesterday that Beth comes from a family of witches, and the three guys are all shifters of some sort, so I don't have to worry about what craziness they may see in the store. Even if they were human, they wouldn't see the insane shit because of the wards in the town, but I need people that can see the insane shit because there is a lot of it to deal with. I listen to their overview of yesterday, happy to hear that Lars went over all the basics with them. They can clean cages, feed animals, give them some much-needed attention, and Beth can even run the cash register. I think they'll be a great fit here with us, and they seem to really enjoy the time spent with all the animals, which is the most important part.

I watch as Landyn goes straight to cleaning bird cages, accidentally letting a few of the birds out and cursing loudly. Elias flies up and grabs the birds without issue, placing them back in their cages after they have been cleaned. Damian and Rhett play with Klaus, whose rash seems to be getting much better. Everything feels comfortable and perfect, except for the sick feeling I have in my stomach about Lars not coming in. I sent him a few text messages to check on him, but didn't get a reply. I tap my nails on the counter as the sick feeling refuses to go away.

We work through the day, and everything gets done so much faster with all the helping hands. I go through the inventory and get more cat trees and dog beds ordered, speak with some of my favorite customers, and get lots of cuddles in with Klaus. But the whole day goes by with no word from Lars.

After Beth, Rob, and Dakota leave and I begin closing the store, I look at my phone one last time and feel my heart drop when I see there are still no messages. "I'm really worried about Lars," I tell the guys.

"Could he be mad that you've been absent so much?

Maybe he wanted a day off, so he just took it?" Damian says logically, but it still doesn't feel right.

"I just don't think he'd leave the store empty all day, especially with how flighty I've been lately. He wouldn't let the animals suffer just to make a point."

Rhett puts his arms around me, pulling me close. "If you're worried, we can stop by his house. See if he's okay."

I nod, biting my lip in thought. I've been a really shitty friend and co-worker lately, but I just know that he wouldn't abandon the animals. Something has to have happened. We walk out into the darkness and over to Landyn's SUV, and I toss him the keys, as my stomach feels like it's in knots. "You drive, I'll give directions. I'm too nervous."

We drive through the darkness, exiting town and heading down the backroads that lead into the bear community north of town. The trees out here are crowded together, making the darkness seem much worse than it is. Landyn's headlights shine brightly in front of us as he drives slowly, on the lookout for wild animals and shifters out on their nightly runs.

"Lars lives out here?" Rhett asks, leaning forward between Landyn and me.

"Yup, right on the edge of the bear community. He lives by himself, since he doesn't interact with the rest of the clan much, but he always stays close to the community for his family."

"This is where Rhett was attacked, about a mile or so that way," Damian says thoughtfully, and I remember him telling me that the night we met. That they were running out by the bear community outside of town.

"Do you think the brothers come out here often? Maybe they took him?" Fear claws through me, and I grab onto Landyn's hand. "It's just up here, please hurry."

When Landyn puts the SUV in park, I leap out of it and run towards Lars' door, but I don't see anyone around. His door is slightly ajar, and none of the lights are on inside. I push the door open in a rush, reaching for the light switch. As light floods the room, a scream leaves my throat as I take in the room around me. Several animals lie on the floor, unmoving, with the familiar black smoke wafting from their open mouths.

My blood runs cold as I walk towards the coffee table in the center of the room and see Lars' old dog, Apollo, lying on his back, his legs stiff and his tail, that I always remember wagging crazily, lying limp.

Chapter 33

Calluna

As I rush into the room and drop to Apollo's side, I hear the men run in behind me, their gasps audible in the quiet room. Soundless tears escape me as I put my hands into Apollo's fur, murmuring words of a spell that I hope will help him. I feel a heartbeat pounding in his chest, and the amount of black smoke is less than the others in the room, so I'm hoping that's good news.

"*I call upon the powers far and near.*
To banish the darkness that has resided here.
The moon will awaken,
the sleeping sun.
May the darkness be broken,
may the spell be done."

I chant the words, barely above a breath, with my eyes sealed shut. My hands tingle with the black sparks I felt yesterday outside of Black Moon Magick, and I concentrate on that power.

"*The blood that I spill,*

bends you to my will.
My darkness will reign,
my power you'll gain."

"A knife," I growl, my eyes still tightly shut. I hear movement as I continue to repeat the words, and a knife is placed in my open hand. Opening my eyes, I cut my hand, my blood dribbling into the dog's mouth. I watch in awe as the dog twitches, its eyes flashing open. A sigh of relief exits me just as Apollo jumps from the table and turns to me. Prepared to greet the sweet, excitable dog, I'm thrown when he leaps at me with his teeth bared.

My back hits the floor as Apollo stands above me, his large paws on my chest and his teeth still bared menacingly. His eyes are pure black, the warmness I remember gone. "Calluna!" I hear someone yell, but all I can do is stare at the dog above me.

"Nobody hurt him!" I yell, putting my hand out to stop the men from harming the dog. I slam a hand into the dog's chest, filling it with that same black, electric energy, and throw the animal off my body. "Grab him," I growl to Elias, who's standing closest to the dog. He grabs the thrashing dog and throws it into the nearby bathroom, slamming the door shut behind him and holding the handle to keep the door shut. Apollo growls and barks on the other side, his nails digging into the wood.

"What the fuck was that?" Landyn asks, his eyes wide as he looks around the room. "You're a witch?"

"Yes, kind of," I reply as I stand and stretch my shoulders and back in pain where Apollo slammed me to the ground.

"Fuck, I just thought you were a changeling. You practice dark magic?" Landyn asks, looking around the room. "What happened here?"

"Planning to run again, Lan?" I ask, looking at him in accusation.

Damian comes to my side and rubs his hands down my arms, trying to comfort me. "I think we're all just a little surprised. What you did there was much different than what I saw you do to Rhett. Have you done that spell before?"

"It wasn't that different than what I've done before. I just did what I was pulled to do. Black electricity is new." I shake my hands, closing my eyes. "I don't know what the fuck happened there any more than you do."

Landyn walks up to me and grabs my chin, leveling my eyes with his. "I won't leave you again. You have to trust me. But whatever you did made that dog attack you, and it scared the fuck out of me."

I nod, his fingers still on my chin. "Okay. Right, it's fine. I understand." I look around the room, barely holding in the tears that threaten to spill. "Where the fuck is Lars?"

Rhett and Elias begin searching the rooms in the house as Damian pulls me onto a nearby couch, Landyn taking a seat beside me while eyeing the rest of the animals warily. "What about the rest of these guys? Are they dead?"

I close my eyes, unwilling to look at the rest of the nameless animals scattered around the room. Rhett and Elias re-enter the room, indicating Lars is nowhere to be found, and my heart sinks.

Where is he?

"Luna, I know you won't want to hear this, but is there a possibility that Lars did this?" Damian asks quietly, rubbing his hand against my arm.

I immediately shake my head, opening my eyes and looking into Damian's. "No, I've known him for too long. He would never do this, especially not to Apollo." The sound of the dog snarling in the background, and his missing owner make me feel numb.

"Okay, sweetheart, I believe you. We need to call the police and file a missing person's report," he says, standing and helping me up. "Let's go back to the SUV while we wait."

I sit in the backseat, surrounded by Damian and Elias' arms as I cry. After a while, the police arrive, and their red and blue lights flash blurrily through my tears outside the window as I stare at the home of my best friend. I have no idea where he is or whether he's safe. I close my eyes when I can't watch Rhett and Landyn speaking to the officers anymore. Landyn clasps the tall man that I recognize as one of Violet's mates, a troll, on the shoulder before turning towards the vehicle and looking at us sadly.

I wake up in the morning in my own bed, Rhett and Elias on each side of me, Landyn asleep in a chair in the corner. My eyes ache from crying and feel gritty from the tears that dried there in my sleep. I look around the room, unsure where Damian is, until I see a small note next to my cell phone.

I went to open the store for Beth and the boys. We'll care for the animals, then I'll be back home to you, mi Luna.

My throat feels tight as I read the note, and feel overwhelming emotions at the care that he has shown me. That they all have shown me. I look over to the chair in the corner and see Landyn watching me. "Good morning, Callie." His voice is thick with sleep.

I slowly crawl out of bed, trying to avoid waking my other two sleeping mates, and walk across the room to

Landyn. He pulls me into his lap, and I worry for my old chair at holding both our weights, though Landyn seems unworried. "Did you sleep here all night?" I ask, dragging my fingers down the side of his cheek and his short beard.

"There wasn't much sleeping, but yes, I stayed here all night," he replies with a small smile, his large arms holding me close to him.

"Why didn't you sleep on the couch if there was no room on the bed?" I ask, putting my head on his shoulder.

"I didn't want to be away from you, baby. I meant what I said, I don't want to leave your side again," he tells me seriously, his sincerity shining in his chestnut brown eyes. "I wouldn't say no to a larger bed though. A king-size is great, but it's a bit small for five people."

I giggle at the ridiculousness of that phrase and that I now have four men sleeping in my bed. Four! How the fuck did we end up here? The thought brings me back to Lars' comment about this not being what he meant by living a little. Sadness once again tears at my chest.

"I want to go to Black Moon Magick. Speak to the brothers," I state resolutely, looking at Landyn and daring him to say no.

"Isn't that who you think is doing all this?" he asks dejectedly. "The guys filled me in last night on what I've missed. Do you think we should really just bust into that place, guns blazing?"

"Yes. If they're doing this, then they're our best bet at finding Lars. Wake up the guys for me, please? I'm going to go call Damian and tell him my plan. He's at my shop, so he can meet us there," I tell Landyn as I walk out of the room with my cellphone in hand. *I'm coming, Lars.*

Chapter 34

Calluna

The text messages from Damian make me all too aware that he isn't a fan of this idea, and after Landyn fills in Elias and Rhett, it's clear that they don't think much of it either. None of them try to argue with me though, and I'm grateful. They just get dressed resolutely and rally behind me.

I concentrate on the black ball of energy that I've felt in my chest since I started really doing magic. Maybe it comes from my changeling nature, or maybe something else. All I know is that after yesterday with Elias, it has felt stronger. Like claiming the last of my four men flipped something on inside me, or maybe that's just romantic bullshit filling my head. But in a reality where I have fated mates based on a magical book, who am I to deny magic-spurring semen?

I tie my hair into a bun on the top of my head, feeling much happier when it's out of my face and off my shoulders, and tell the guys I'm ready. Kick ass or not, I'm doing this. Deciding to walk, I send a text message to Damian, telling him we are on our way, and we walk the couple blocks to Black Moon Magick.

"So, what's the plan here?" Rhett asks, walking beside me. "Black magic and ninja kicks? I'm pretty fast, but I don't know how I'll do against two elves that know magic." He jabs me in the side, hoping to pull a laugh from me, and I can't help but give him a small smile. I'm too filled with nervous energy to truly find anything funny right now, but his cuteness is just too much to ignore.

"Honestly, I have no idea," I say with a sigh. I'm worried that I could be walking myself—and my men—into a situation that will end in all of us being badly hurt. But not dead, right? They can't just kill five people in the middle of town, right? "Am I being stupid?"

"It feels rash, that is for certain. But no, *mi alma*, you are not stupid," Elias comforts me as he grabs my hand, squeezing it tightly. "Besides, you have your magic and four men behind you that would do anything for you. A griffin, a fallen angel, a fox, and a meerkat. Your very own clan of misfits."

"I always did have a thing for the underdog," I reply with a sigh.

I pick up my pace when I see the shop and notice that the door is propped open. I run inside and find two police officers—Liam, Violet's troll mate from the night before, and another man I don't recognize already speaking to Damian. Damian smiles at me weakly, looking nervous.

"This is official police business. The store is closed," the unknown cop says to me, standing between us and the rest of the store.

"It's okay, Bert. They're the reason we're here," Liam says with a kind smile. "Have you heard from your friend?"

"No," I state in annoyance, glaring up at Bert. "Have you

guys figured anything out?" I quirk a brow at the man in front of me in challenge. Rhett grabs my shoulders and pulls me back gently.

"The brothers we were told about last night seem to be a dead-end," Bert says, looking at me. "No dead animals, no traces of anything unusual. No evidence of them cursing animals. The only evidence we have of animals being cursed is what we saw at your friend's house last night. Have you considered your friend," he pauses to consult a notepad, "Larson Monticello, might be doing all this, and now he skipped town?"

"Isn't it suspicious that they aren't here? That they fled before they could be questioned by you guys?" I snap, glaring at the men.

Bert purses his lips. "I could say the same about your friend. History with the law." He flips through his notepad. "Multiple street fights. Several counts of public intoxication and public indecency..."

"Oh, for fuck's sake. How does that matter in this situation?" I spit back.

"Most *recently*, a reliable source has informed us that he has been storing a large number of unknown crates in his truck, which are also missing. Not odd, as he works closely with you in your shop, but based on the look on your face, I'm going to assume you know nothing about the crates?" Bert goes on while staring down at me. "All we have from the brothers is this note, that makes absolutely no sense. But what we have on Larson is a lot more. I know that two elven brothers moving into town and opening a dark magic shop make them easy scapegoats, but I honestly can't ignore the number of cursed animals turning up in your shop and the amount found at your best friend's home."

"What source?" I hiss. "What makes them so reliable?"

"Officer Brown. It's good having a bear on the force in situations like these."

"Bert is just doing his job," Liam says as anger flashes in my eyes, and probably I look like I'm about to claw his eyes out.

I give him a forced smile. "Where is this note?"

Liam looks at me uneasily before walking to the counter, grabbing the paper, and handing it to me. "I probably shouldn't be showing you this."

I roll my eyes. "Yeah, yeah. Our little secret."

I look down at the thin letters scrawled onto the sheet of paper.

Remember, everyone is curious about the dark side of magic, even if they are unwilling to admit it. It's addictive in its nature. It is exotic and seductive. Before you know it, you are just practicing magic with no regard to the light or dark qualities.

I recognize the words from our first conversation, and I grit my teeth, angry at myself for ever trusting the man. My eyes drop to the last words written towards the bottom.

All is not what it seems, everything is continually changeling. The place of the mate's attack is the key.

So mote it be.

My heart freezes as I read the word *changeling* in place of changing, knowing that wasn't an error. My hand not holding the note clenches into a fist, and I try to hold myself together. To not show any emotion in the presence of Liam and Bert.

"Can I take this?" I ask Liam, pleading with my eyes.

"Absolutely not," Bert interjects, looking at me in disbelief.

"Ugh, fine," I say, pulling my phone out and snapping a picture. "Thanks, you guys! Gotta run!"

"I miss the good old days," I hear Bert say to Liam as I dash out of the store.

"One of these days, you'll get a smartphone, too. I'm betting on it," Liam laughs.

Chapter 35

Calluna

I rush out of the store with my men following behind me. I stare at the words on my phone, reading them over and over. *The place of the mate's attack is the key.*

"Rhett? Damian?" I ask aloud, finally prying my eyes from my phone. "Can you take me to the place Rhett was attacked?"

Damian grabs my arm, stopping me from speed walking any farther. "What is going on, Luna? What did the note say?" He looks into my eyes as if trying to read my mind through their depths.

"Not here," I say, looking around. "Let's get to Lan's SUV. I'll explain on the way."

Damian just nods to me, and we all walk quickly back to my apartment building and into the parking garage to get Landyn's SUV. Elias jumps in the passenger seat, and Landyn starts it up, pulling out quickly. I sit squeezed between Damian and Rhett, staring at the words on my phone.

"What does 'so mote it be' mean?" Rhett asks, reading over my shoulder.

"It's an old Wiccan phrase. It means 'so must it be' in the literal sense. Those who pray to the god and goddess end with that, sort of like the Christian 'amen.' This note is directed to me. Look at where he uses the word 'changeling' instead of changing and mentions the 'mate's attack,'" I explain, anxiety swirling in my chest. "I told him about your attack and all the cursed animals, but never that you were my mate. I don't think."

"How would he know?" Damian asks, worry laced in his tone.

"No idea," I say, my mouth dry. We pull into Rhett and Damian's driveway, and Landyn shuts off the engine. I start pushing Damian to get out of the car so we can get to the spot.

"Luna, this seems like a trap. We have no idea what could be waiting for us there. They could ambush us on sight, and then we'll be no use to Lars," Damian pleads, blocking my way to the door.

"Damien, I have to try. I can't just sit back and wait to see if the police will or even *can* do anything," I beg. Rhett opens his door, pulling me out with him, and I hear Damien sigh in defeat. "Bikes?" I ask Rhett, and he nods, running over to their shed.

"We only have the two," he says, looking to Elias and Landyn.

"Don't worry, we can fly," Landyn says, his eyes flashing gold as his griffin stirs within him. Elias nods in agreement, his large, black wings spreading out behind him.

"Okay, let's do this then," Rhett says, pulling his bike out as Damian does the same begrudgingly. I watch as Landyn shifts into his griffin form, his head almost level with my own and coming to Elias' shoulders. His huge, black wings expand to the same width as Elias'. Standing proudly, his head shakes slightly as he looks at me. The darkness of his griffin leads me to believe that it would be almost invisible at night, and I marvel at the beauty of his form.

Elias jumps off the ground, his wings flapping with a large gust of wind as he flies into the sky. With Landyn at his side, they look down at us, waiting for Rhett and Damian to lead the way. I hop onto Rhett's bike, knowing he'll drive the fastest, and we're off. We fly through the trees quickly, branches stinging as they whip across my cheeks, and I put my face against Rhett's back.

The forest rushes past me in a blur, and I close my eyes, trying to concentrate on the black ball of energy in my chest. Can I do this? Maybe, maybe not. But I have to try. I think of all the animals that have been brought into my shop with that black smoke leaking from their mouths. I think of Apollo and the fury in his eyes, and I hope I can fix him. I think of Klaus, Jake, Nina, Binx, and every single pet that has taken a place in my heart. My home for misfit pets, and the man that has helped me every step of the way. *Lars*. Not for a second do I believe that he did this. There's no way.

The bike slows as we pull into the area, and I see the two elven men kneeling on the ground, their wrists bound in black, glowing magic, their lips tightly closed. A deep, bloody cut mars Nelcar's cheek, and he looks at me with malice. Falcar's eyes widen when we approach, then close slowly as if in regret. Beside them, lying on the ground motionless, I see Lars. His red plaid shirt is unbuttoned and ripped in places, a giant gash down the center of his chest. Dried blood coats his skin, and his eyes are closed. His face is covered in bruises and cuts, his lip split. I jump off the bike, not waiting for Rhett to stop, and rush towards Lars' motionless body just as I hear my men yell behind me.

A chorus of 'no' and 'Calluna' echo behind me as a towering man steps out of the tall brush. His long, gray-white hair is pushed back on the top and flows across his back and shoulders. His skin is such a dark gray that it appears almost black. His features are all rigid, from his thin, pointed nose to his high, sharp cheekbones. Two blood-red eyes sit below arched white eyebrows, and his sharp, white teeth smile at me evilly as he raises his hand and mutters unheard words.

My body goes cold and rigid as I'm pulled off my feet and into the air. I hover above the ground, my eyes welling with tears as pain lashes through my body. My throat burns from a soundless scream as I watch the man with black magic hit Damian, who then falls to the ground. Barely able to breathe, my heart stutters as I watch the rest of my men roar in anger, rushing toward the man. Elias goes to grab me, but screams in pain as he's electrified when his fingers touch my skin. Then he drops to the ground, as motionless as Lars.

Landyn flies towards the dark elf, his sharp talons glinting in the sunlight as they swipe at the man, the sound of his griffin's screech echoing in the forest. With a cold laugh, the man swipes his hand, and I watch in horror as Landyn too drops to the ground, followed by Rhett in fox form.

The dark elf steps closer to me and looks up as I hover above him, twitching in pain. "Hello, my daughter. Thank you for joining this lovely *family reunion*," he says in an ice-cold tone, his voice thick with an elven accent. He looks over to Falcar and Nelcar, who kneel on the ground, eyeing me with fear. "I see you have already met your brothers." I work to blink the tears away as I stare into the face of my *father*.

Chapter 36

Calluna

The man that calls himself my father releases his magic, and I crumple to the ground, wincing in pain as my bare legs hit the hard forest floor. What a day to wear shorts. I crawl towards Elias, who lies beside me, and I start shaking him.

"He won't wake," my father says in a cold voice, walking closer to us. "My magic is much stronger than yours."

I look around and see some animals lying lifeless on the ground. They're mostly just wild squirrels and rabbits, but my heart still breaks for them. "Magic that you choose to use on defenseless animals?" I spit out, wincing in pain as I shift to stand.

"How else could I lure my animal-loving *changeling* daughter to me?" he says in a flat tone. "Small curses here and there, enough to awaken your dark magic. To encourage you to begin practicing, to strengthen the darkness inside you."

"You did all this to get to me?" I ask, feeling sick to my

stomach. All those animals...their lives ruined, all because of me.

"Of course. I knew that you would need to get to the bottom of it, but it seems you got distracted by a bit of *mate magic*." He says the words in disgust, eyeing my men scattered around us. "Too bad the fates didn't pick stronger men for you. They were taken down far too easily." He walks over and kicks Damian's side.

"Stop!" I growl, feeling the black energy radiating inside me, electricity sparking off my fingertips. He nudges Rhett, my tiny fox shifter still in fox form, shooting a bolt of magic into him and watching as he morphs back into a man. "I said, STOP!" My voice comes out in a roaring growl, and I throw a hand forward, black magic sparking from my fingertips and hurtling through the air between us. It collides with his chest and throws him to the ground.

He immediately stands, his eyes wide, a deranged smile on his lips. "You are much stronger than I thought. This is good. *Very good*."

"Wake them," I demand, and he laughs a cold, cruel laugh.

"Now why would I do that?"

My annoyance flares, and I push another spark of magic at him, but he easily deflects it. "What do you want from me?"

"I want you to join me, daughter. Once your brothers become compliant, then we will truly be unstoppable. I've been hanging around here for a while, watching you. I even started up a *relationship* with your best friend so that I could get more information on you. Posed as a mad scientist that was looking to discover more about supernatural gifts, creating helpful spells and such. I even would send the animals I cursed with Larson and other people in town to bring to you." He looks over at my best friend lying on the ground. "Such a stupid, stupid man. He never suspected me and respected my wishes about keeping our relationship a secret. His only redeemable quality is that he is awfully good at sucking cock."

I force down a sick feeling, bitterness filling my mouth at his words. How long had he been orchestrating everything behind the scenes? Manipulating my best friend? "If I go with you, will you let them go? Lars, Elias, Damian, Rhett, and Landyn? Will you let my brothers go?"

I look back and see Falcar shaking his head at me, fear in his eyes. Nelcar just stares at me, his eyes closing as he looks down. I crease my brows, then look back up at my father, awaiting his answer.

"I will let your friend go, as he is of no use to me anymore. Your men...well, I can't be sure they won't follow us. Your brothers, they must come with us. I need all of my children with me. Only then will we be at our strongest." He looks back to them, shaking his head. "They are strong, but stubborn. I *will* bend them to my will."

My lip twitches in anger, my hands clenching into fists. "What makes you think I won't attack you the first chance I get?"

"I think I've made it clear that I am much stronger than you. That I could kill your mates and friend without a second thought." He smiles, shaking his head. "No, you will be compliant if you know what's good for you."

I growl out my frustration, stepping backward as I unleash a large ball of magic at him. He steps to the side with a bitter laugh, once again avoiding the magic. Just as I'd hoped. The magic hits Falcar, wrapping around the magic binding his wrists and releasing the binds. He flexes his hands before sending gray sparks into the bindings on Nelcar's wrists.

Our father's eyes never leave mine as he steps towards me quickly, his hand going to my throat and pinning me against a tree. "You will not disobey me, child," he spits out, magic flowing through the fingers he squeezes tightly around my throat. I feel my vision change as my eyes go black, a pinch as my ears lengthen to points, and my skin igniting as it changes its color. My fingers clutch at his wrist, tearing at his skin in an attempt to get him to release me. "There she is. My changeling daughter. I knew creating you wasn't the abomination that your feeble mother believed. Your darkness should be embraced, not hidden behind this human façade. Though I have envied the changeling's ability to blend in with the humans. Much easier to hide when you don't have the face of an elf."

Out of the corner of my eye, I see Falcar pulling Nelcar to stand, and then both men close their eyes, hands grasped together. My vision feels blurry as I struggle for air, and my father's words go unheard to my ears as my body lacks oxygen. My eyes fall to my mates who lie unmoving on the ground, to Lars' immobile form. I blink slowly, a tear sliding down my cheek as my eyes connect back to the blinding red of my father's. The last face I will see as he slowly chokes me to death for my defiance. His eyes widen perceptibly as his grip releases from my throat, and I shudder as my body hits the ground. My eyes zero in on the bright white light radiating from our father's chest.

Falcar walks towards me, his hand reaching out and grasping mine, helping me up. His gray magic flows through me, and I feel lighter, the pain inflicted upon me lessening. Falcar looks to Nelcar with a pointed look, and Nelcar grabs my hand begrudgingly, squeezing slightly at the connection. White magic radiates from his hands as gray radiates from Falcar's. Both seem to stream into me, connecting with my own and making my chest feel as if it could explode. Our father looks up at us in fear as my two brothers murmur words foreign to my ears, and then my eyes are forced closed. His cries echo in the forest as blinding pain radiates through me, scorching me to my bones. My body becomes rigid, and I scream out in pain, feeling as if razors are slicing through my skin. Their foreign dialect becomes a chanting in my head as I become dizzy from the pain. An extreme ache settles over my muscles, and my skull feels as if it's being cracked apart. My eyes fly open, and I watch in horror as our father's body hovers above the ground, cracks spreading over his skin emitting white, gray, and black smoke. I shudder as I watch his form explode into a puff of smoke, his screams echoing in my ears like nails down a chalkboard.

When everything goes black and my hands feel suddenly empty, I gasp at air that seems to do nothing but choke me. The taste of my mates' names on my tongue soothe me into what I can only imagine is my everlasting sleep.

Landyn.
Damian.
Rhett.
Elias.
En la oscuridad Brillas. Mis salvadores.

Chapter 37

Calluna

I wake up to gentle shaking and warm arms tightly holding me to a hard chest. Blinking my eyes, I look up into the flecked copper eyes of Elias, who smiles at me gently. I turn my head to the side slowly, my neck feeling stiff, and jerk wildly when I notice that the ground is far below us.

"Holy fuck!" I yell, clutching at Elias in terror as his arms tighten around me, and he chuckles softly.

"Good morning, *mi alma*," he says through a laugh.

"W-We're fucking flying," I stutter nervously, looking down at the ground and feeling my heart drop to my stomach.

"We are," he agrees as his large, black wings flap behind him. I look over to see Landyn flying next to us in his griffin form with his legs curled into his body and his powerful wings gliding through the air easily. "We are going to the store where we met, Black Moon Magick. The elf brothers, they claim to be your brothers?" he asks me skeptically, his eyes searching my face.

"They are. It was my father that did this," I say, then my lips twist into a frown. "Lars, where is he?" I ask in fear, my breaths quickening.

"He is fine. Falcar and Nelcar were able to wake him, along with the rest of us. Rhett took him on one of the bikes, and they will meet us in Landyn's truck."

I nod and cuddle into Elias' chest, my body still feeling achy. When we land gently on the ground, Elias places me back on my feet and keeps a hand on my back to steady me. I walk into the store to find Nelcar and Falcar sitting on chairs in the back, looking a little worse for wear.

"Why didn't you tell me you were my brothers?" I ask Falcar, then bite the inside of my lip.

Falcar's lips form a tight frown, and Nelcar grimaces. "Would you have believed me?" Falcar asks as he rubs some sort of salve on a cut on his arm. "You entered this store already distrusting me."

"I probably wouldn't have," I agree with a sigh.

"I came here knowing that our father was looking for you. When you told me about the cursed animals and your mate being cursed, I knew it must be him. I called upon Nelcar, who came reluctantly, having spent all of his life avoiding any type of run-in with our father. I knew that we had to protect you from him, that his goal of collecting his powerful children had to be stopped." As Falcar says the words, and I look to Nelcar in surprise, my body feels numb. Someone who seems to outwardly hate me came here to help me, even though it meant he might have to face our father?

"Why? Why was he trying to collect us?"

"For our magic. To get us to work with him against his

enemies. Elrohir is not a friend to the Elven court, and he has many that oppose his use of dark magic," Nelcar says snidely.

"For someone that came here to help me, you seem to really fucking hate me," I spit out at Nelcar, and he smiles. The first smile I've seen on the man's face.

"I was raised to despise changelings, so you will have to forgive my predisposition. I am trying to overcome it," he replies. "I also don't take too kindly to people barging in and blaming me for things I had nothing to do with."

"That raven I saw you two doing magic on—" I start, only to be interrupted by Nelcar.

"We were removing the curse," he spits out, then whistles loudly. The large, black raven flies into the room and lands on his shoulder. "You are not the only one that likes animals, *sister*."

I frown and nod, feeling foolish. "I'm sorry that I blamed you both."

"It's easy to blame elves, especially ones that are believed to be dark magic wielders," Falcar replies dismissively.

"Is he dead?" I ask as I remember him bursting into the same black smoke that I would find within the cursed animals.

"Probably not. He is very strong, and I doubt that what we did was enough to truly kill him. Perhaps we only disabled him, until he is able to gain enough power to come back," Falcar replies thoughtfully.

Nelcar frowns, nodding his head in agreement. "Evil is not so easily disposed of."

I hear Landyn's SUV pull up, and I run outside. Lars steps from the vehicle, dried blood coating his bare chest. I leap into his arms, embracing him and pulling a gasp of pain from his lips.

"I'm sorry," I say and drop from his arms. I hold onto him and look him over as tears fill my eyes at the knowledge of what he went through. "I am so sorry, Lars."

"Hey, stop that," he says, pulling me back into his chest. "This isn't your fault. If anything, it's mine. I don't know how I let myself get tied up with that man."

"He's my father," I sob and hide my face in his chest.

"Yeah, so I've heard. He's also been my boyfriend for months." He drags a hand down his face. "This is all so *fucked up*."

"Yeah, it is," I reply with a sad smile. "Let's not talk about it. I'm just *so* glad you're okay."

"Same, Cal," he says, and squeezes me tightly. "I'm going to get a ride home from Landyn. I need sleep, and from what I hear, my house is a disaster."

"Apollo?" I ask, my voice wavering.

"We fixed him last night. That's where Elrohir found us," Falcar says as he puts a comforting hand on my shoulder. I smile at him, my eyes still filled with tears as I mouth my thanks.

"Take me home on the way to Lars'?" I ask, looking to Landyn. He nods and pulls me into his arms, then walks me to his SUV and puts me in the back.

Chapter 38

Calluna

A few days pass with the guys handling me with kid gloves. Falcar and Nelcar work with me, trying to remove the rest of the traces from the curses on the animals in the shop, but not all of them can be removed. Jake, Lina, and Binx are stuck with their traces, though I now see them more as quirks. Klaus' rash is completely removed, and he has been adopted by my brothers. I've been trying to form relationships with them, but it's still very strained between us. Lots of distrust on both sides, but a work in progress. The constant fear of my father's reappearance encourages me to work to further my magical abilities, so Nelcar teaches me light magic and Falcar helps with dark. I hope to become as powerful as they are, and I'm already seeing huge improvements.

I lie in my bed which has grown considerably, though not due to magic. At some point, Landyn purchased a California king and put it in my room. It's so large, it pretty much goes from wall to wall in my small, one-bedroom apartment. I feel much better with all my men lying with me in it, though. I chuckle a bit as I finish reading *Love Blooms* by C. C. Pine. I decided that the book that gave me my mates deserved to be finished, even if I think it's a bit silly.

"What are you laughing at, beautiful?" Rhett asks, leaning on the doorframe of my bedroom.

"It's just a sweet book. The flower shifter gets her princes," I say whimsically.

"Flower shifter?" he says with a smile, and I laugh.

"Yup, complete with flower underwear."

"Well, that sounds itchy." He leaps on me, pinning me to the bed and pressing a kiss to my lips. I shift beneath him, feeling the heat pool between my thighs. Part of the whole kid gloves act has included no sex, which is driving me insane. How did I go from fucking four deliciously sexy guys, to sleeping in a bed with them all and no touching? I'm so sexually frustrated, even my dreams have become raunchy, and I'm begging for some dick-lash.

I feel Rhett's cock stiffen between us, and I smile up at him. "Seems like someone wants to play," I purr, moving my hand down to cup his hardness.

His face becomes strained, and he grabs both my hands, pinning them above my head. "Don't, beautiful," he rasps.

"Why not?" I pout, wigging my core against him again and prying another groan from his all too sexy lips.

"Because we're alone, and I promised the guys," he replies, his eyes tortured.

"Promised them what?" I snap and squint my eyes at him in accusation.

"That we'd give you a second to chill. You went from no mates to four mates within a couple of days, then you were tortured by your father who was also torturing your best friend. You watched said father attack your mates, then you and your newfound brothers magicked him into a puff of smoke, and he's probably still out there, all Voldemort-like, plotting his revenge," he explains, and I pinch my lips together to avoid smiling. "What could you possibly find funny about all that?" he asks, his own smile appearing.

"That my father is Voldemort-like." I giggle. "Is it too much to ask for a little normality? I mean, I have all this glorious cock being flaunted around my house, and I'm finally ready to ride some. So just *give me* what I want," I growl and grind my core against him once more.

"Fuck," he groans, his cock twitching against me. "Beautiful, you're killing me. Landyn and Damian are both working, and Elias is asleep on the couch. I *promised*."

"No, he's not." A deep voice draws my attention to the door, and I see Elias standing there with a smile. "What's going on here? Hmmm? I thought we were waiting."

"I'm trying. She's killing me," Rhett groans, looking over his shoulder at my fallen angel.

"Oh, I'm sure she is, the little minx." Elias chuckles darkly as he moves onto the bed, and places kisses along my neck.

"Not you too," Rhett groans as I grind into him more, spurred on by Elias' lips on me.

"I texted Landyn and Damian, '*the times are a changeling.*' They'll be here soon," Elias says against my throat, causing my body to shiver.

"How very Bob Dylan of you," I say breathily as Rhett joins in on the torture and rubs his hardness into my core. Elias moves to kiss my lips, and his tongue drags against the seam, begging for entry. He delves in, using one of my moans to gain entrance, and his tongue explores me thoroughly. Rhett keeps his grip tight on my wrists and begins kissing my neck, traveling lower to the tops of my breasts peeking out above my tank top. Changing to grip my wrists with one hand, he uses the other to pull down my top and release one of my breasts. My nipple pebbles in the cool air, and he bends to swirl his tongue around the bud before placing tender kisses all over the skin. I moan into Elias' mouth and feel his hardness against my side.

Breaking our kiss, Elias shifts lower and grabs the sides of my leggings and lace panties, his arms pushing Rhett to the side. He pulls down both painstakingly slowly, only revealing an inch of skin at a time and making me quiver in anticipation. Pulling the clothing off my ankles, he throws them across the room, and they hit the wall and fall to the floor. His fingers slowly graze up my legs and are followed by his lips placing gentle kisses, his scruffy beard prickling my sensitive skin. He moves his fingers slowly across my sex, just grazing the top and driving me wild as I thrust into his hand, begging for more pressure. He chuckles darkly against my neck as I squirm, and his hot breaths tickle me. Rhett pulls me forward and tugs my shirt up and over my head, exposing both of my breasts and giving him more access.

I moan loudly as Elias moves back down my body, leveling his face with my core and pushing my legs up and over his shoulders. I shudder beneath him as his hot breath touches my sensitive area, just before he drags his tongue from bottom to top. I tense beneath him as his tongue works gently, delving slightly into my entrance, then moving back up to circle my clit. "More," I beg, needing more pressure, or his fingers—something more than the gentle touches they're giving me.

He kisses my pussy slowly, savoring each lick and stroke, taking his time with me. His fingers dig into my ass as he holds my pussy to his mouth.

I hear a noise and look up to see Landyn standing at the door, his eyes hooded. "Glad to see I'm not too late." He licks his lips slowly as he watches Elias eat my pussy. "Damian is here too. I saw him parking his car on my way in."

My voice comes out in a loud squeak as Elias nibbles on my clit, drawing my attention back to him. "Fuuuuuuuck," I groan as I feel myself becoming more tightly wound. Then the bed dips, and Landyn pulls his body up to mine to lick at the nipples that Rhett has left wanting. I hear the door open and close, then Damian has joined us in a flash, obviously running the whole way.

"Jeez, you'd think you guys were all about to lose your virginities," I joke around a moan as Elias slips a slick finger into my entrance.

"Being in a house with you and giving you space is the definition of blue balls," Damian says and then kisses me roughly, then he moves to kiss Rhett. The two slam their mouths together and grab roughly at each other's faces. I watch in fucking horny glee as they make love to each other's mouths, their cocks hardening in their pants, just as Elias pushes in a second finger and sucks hard on my clit. I scream out my release, my own fingers digging into the sheets below me as I feel my core squeezing at Elias' fingers. Landyn swallows my screams by plunging his tongue into my mouth, his hand roughly gripping one of my breasts.

Rhett and Damian begin quickly undressing each other, and I can't take my eyes off them. Muscle against muscle, hardness against hardness, they come together, and I can't help but marvel at the fucking beauty of it.

"Come here, *mi Luna*," Damian growls, pulling me onto my knees and between them. Their hard cocks brush against my skin, the tips wet with pre-cum. They work me over, one on each side, kissing down the column of my neck to my breasts. Damian's large hand slaps at my ass, then he rubs and squeezes at the area. I throw my head back as Rhett's fingers slip down to drag through my wetness, and he pinches my sensitive clit.

"I want you to fuck me, Rhett," I moan, and his eyes blaze as I say the words. I drag my nails slowly down his chest, causing him to shiver, and I smile evilly, prepared to torture these men now. "And I want Damian to take you from behind while you fuck me."

"Fuck, yes," Damian growls, his cock twitching against me. I turn to lie back down, then pull Rhett between my legs and level his cock with my entrance. I shudder in eagerness when I hear the lid of the bottle of lube from my nightstand popping open, then watch Damian squirt a generous amount into his palm and drag it slowly up and down his cock. Rhett pushes into me, and I suck in a quick breath, thoroughly enjoying the stretch of his thick cock. His forehead comes to mine, and I look into his eyes and see the exact moment that Damian penetrates him, as his eyes flare with pleasure. His guttural moan pairing with Damian's has me squirming beneath them, needing friction on my needy clit.

"Elias," I moan out, looking for my fallen angel. "I want to taste you." I bite my lip as he moves closer to me, and his cock bounces into my vision, looking painfully hard. I grip the base, squeezing gently and pulling a heavy sigh from his lips. I pull him towards me until the tip is just inches away from my lips, and I blow out lightly. I watch as his thick thighs tighten in front of me, then his fingers come down to lace in my hair, urging me toward him. I smile, then pause as a soft moan leaves my lips when Damian slams into Rhett, causing his pelvis to grind against my clit.

Elias groans loudly as his fingers pull at my hair, causing

feelings of pleasure-pain from the pricks at my scalp. "Fuck, *mi alma*. Please do not torture me. *Te necesito tan malo.*"

"*Tómalo mi amor*," I whisper to him in Spanish, even though I rarely speak it since leaving my human parents. I drag my tongue against the tip, then move to flick it against the underside of his sensitive head. "*Toma tu placer de mi.*"

His eyes burn brightly at my words, and I loosen my throat, allowing him to fuck my mouth. My fingers clutch at Rhett's shoulders as he rides me into oblivion, and Damian fucks me with Rhett's cock. I moan as Landyn's fingers move to my clit, circling the needy bundle, and I feel my climax approaching rapidly. Rhett groans loudly, and I feel his cock begin pulsing inside me as his hot cum shoots inside me. His orgasm pushes Damian and I over the edge, and my screams of pleasure are muffled around Elias' cock as that too begins pulsing in my mouth. I greedily swallow every drop of his cum, licking every inch of his cock as he pulls it from my mouth, then I look up at him, delirious with pleasure. Damian kisses the back of Rhett's neck as his cock slips from the other man's ass, and they move away from between my legs. I immediately miss their warmth, until it's replaced by my quiet griffin shifter, who's been silently watching the show.

"Hello, baby girl," Landyn breathes, his eyes flashing the gold of his griffin's as he looks me over. He crushes his lips to mine, and I gasp as I feel his cock drag against me, my pussy immediately ready for more. "I felt that I should wait, let the others take their pleasure first. To give you pleasure first. Not keeping you when I should've is something that I'll always regret. I made you wait for me to pull my head out of my ass, but they didn't. I'll *forever* be trying to make that up to you." He pauses, his words making little cracks in my heart as I look up at him, then I gasp as he presses the head of his cock to my entrance. Even with the mixture of my cum and Rhett's, he has to wait for me to adjust to his width, since his cock is the thickest of my men's. The pleasure is pushing me to thrust up and drive him deeper. To give me the friction I so desperately crave.

His eyes never leave mine as he pushes into me in a torturously slow progression, and his voice rasps as he goes on, "Because you, baby girl, deserve everything that we have to give. Every single piece of us." I gasp as he bottoms out, hitting the most sensitive place inside me as he begins to slowly pump in and out. "I promise that you now have every piece of my heart and soul. I'm completely yours, and I'll *never* leave your side again."

My heart cracks, and my vision clouds as tears well in my eyes. "I love you, Landyn," I choke out as my legs wrap around his waist to push him deeper inside me. "Now take me, hard and fast, because I'm yours."

My orgasms begin to cloud together as they all shower me with love, taking every ounce of pleasure from my body. They surround me in their light, embracing my darkness.

Epilogue

We walk into the tattoo parlor in town, Lady Blue Tattoo, and I jump on a large, blue plush couch in the sitting room while Landyn sits down beside me. "Your first tattoo," he says thoughtfully, dragging a finger along the exposed top of my breast. "What do you think you'll be getting?"

I pinch my lips together, trying to hide a smile. "You aren't getting it out of me. It's going to be a surprise." I point to the rest of my men threateningly. "Now all of you zip it."

They laugh out loud, and Damian puts his hands up in innocence. I watch as they each sit down in the various chairs in the large room and I jump up to flip through the designs displayed along the walls.

"None of you have told me what you guys are getting." I pout, looking over to Rhett with my bottom lip pushed out.

"You have your secrets and we have ours, beautiful," Rhett says pointedly, causing me to stick my tongue out at him. I watch as a perky, platinum blonde woman stands behind the counter, and gives care instructions to a large man with a sleeve tattoo on his right arm. The man is almost completely tattooed from head to toe and it seems like he is determined to fill all the empty space, what little is left at least. I go back to sit with my men and my legs immediately start bouncing in anxiety and it feels like sweat is now trickling down my spine.

"Nervous?" Elias asks, pulling me into his side. Landyn groans and puts his hand on my thigh so that he's still touching some part of me. My poor griffin shifter constantly has anxiety running through him and seems to find comfort in my touch. It makes my heart flutter a little knowing that I can bring him such comfort. I wink at him saucily and he just smiles and shakes his head as his hand tightens on my thigh.

"*Mi Luna*, settle down. You're running a mile a minute," Damian teases from across the coffee table between us, watching as I nervously bounce and flip through magazine after magazine.

"You'd think you'd be used to getting poked by now," Rhett jokes, then flashes a sexy wink at me.

"Don't be crass, Rhett," Damian scolds, but barely hides a smile.

"If you ever want to poke me again, you'll behave," I say, scrunching my nose at him. I watch the large, tattooed man leave the store and the woman helping him smiles at me warmly. I stand up and begin to walk over to her.

"Stay here," I order the guys, pointing at them threateningly and allowing a small, black spark to pop from my finger. The guys all try to keep straight faces, pretending to be scared, and I laugh loudly. *Shitheads.*

"I'm Calluna. Those four monsters and I are here for our appointment," I say, looking back at the monsters in question.

The woman laughs, and looks over my shoulder at them. "I'm Dahlia. Welcome to Lady Blue Tattoo! I know we spoke about what you wanted on the phone, but do you know what they're getting? If not, I'm sure I can figure out their heart's desire."

"No," I say stubbornly, pinching my lips in annoyance. "They won't tell me. But they also don't know what I'm getting, so shhh," I tell her conspiratorially, making her laugh.

"Perfect," Dahlia replies. "I'll take you, then Gray and Milo can take two of your men." She pauses as if embarrassed. "I'm sorry, that was presumptuous of me."

"Nope, you're right. *They're all mine*," I reply, letting my eyebrows rise and fall meaningfully.

She smiles and points towards the rooms next to the counter. "Well, we have private rooms for the tattooing, so they won't be able to see anything going on. Do you know which two will be going first?"

"Lemme check," I reply with a smile and walk over to the guys. "So which two of you are getting poked first?" I ask flirtily, my lips pursed to hide a smile.

"You know I'm always down for getting poked." Rhett stands, then grabs my hips and pulls me against him forcefully. He presses a hard kiss to my mouth and bites my lip as he pulls away, successfully getting me all hot and bothered before walking behind me and greeting one of the other artists.

I bite my lip, hard, to hide the moan that wants to escape and look over my shoulder to see Rhett clasping the attractive woman's hand. "Hey, sweetheart! I'm Rhett."

"Gray," the woman with half a wolf tattooed on both arms looks Rhett up and down and winks at him. "Tell me where to poke you, darling."

I shake my head with a slight smile as I look to my other men, raising my brows. "Who else?"

Landyn stands and walks over to me, then places a gentle kiss on my lips. "Elias will go, baby girl. Want me to hold your hand?"

"Yes," I say nervously, looking up into his gorgeous brown eyes. "But no peeking, Lan. I mean it."

"Wouldn't dream of it," he says with a smile as he clutches my hand and allows me to pull him over to the chair. Elias gets up and moves over to sit in the third chair, introducing himself to a hot as sin guy named Milo. Fuck, now I know why it's called Lady Blue Tattoo. This guy is gorgeous enough to give anyone blue ovaries and Gray is all boobs and ass herself.

When we get into the room Dahlia directed us to, my grip tightens on Landyn's hand as she looks at him in question. "He promised to not peek. He's here for moral support."

Sure, it seems fucking silly that in the past few days, I've been attacked by one of my newfound brothers, tortured by my newfound father, then got involved with some freaky fucking magic to reduce said father into a puff a smoke, and yet it's the tattoo that has me sweating. Fear is irrational, *shut up*.

"Okay, take your shirt off and lie down on your chest," Dahlia says as she walks into the room. I pull my shirt off and watch Landyn's eyes dilate as he takes in my purple lace bra, even though he already saw it this morning.

"Where is this tattoo going?" Landyn asks, his voice cracking a bit.

Dahlia smiles reassuringly as she begins getting her tools ready.

"It's on my upper back, just below my neck, but that's all you're getting. Now remember, no peeking!" I tell him with a grin of my own. I have a whole vision of the tattoo I want, something that includes a piece of each of my men. I picked the spot because it turned me on *a lot* to think of one of my men riding me from behind, pulling my hair, my back arched, with the perfect view of the tattoo dedicated to myself and them. Okay, now I've gotten *myself* all hot and bothered. I lie face down and turn my head to the side so I can look at Landyn as it happens.

"Are you ready?" Dahlia asks, turning on the tattoo gun.

"Yes," I reply shakily and squeeze Landyn's hand.

Dahlia immediately gets to work and it hurts a lot less than I thought it would. It's more of a scraping sensation than anything, and once she finishes the outline, I feel myself relaxing more. Landyn's eyes never leave mine, not once. His gaze doesn't move to my back to steal a glance of the tattoo, he just keeps his eyes on me and my heart melts in a puddle. I swear this leather chair will need to be cleaned when we're done. Sweat, tears, possible *excitement*, and now melted heart. *Gross.*

"Do you ever fuck on these chairs?" I ask, standing to marvel at my tattoo in the mirror after she's finished. Landyn turns respectfully, knowing I want to show all the guys at once.

"Um, no. Can't say I have," Dahlia replies with a snicker.

"Are you telling me that you aren't fucking either of those sexy tattoo artists out there?" I gasp, bumping my elbow into her side conspiratorially as she helps me pull my shirt back on.

"Definitely not. Gray is my close friend, and her brother, Milo, is very taken."

I make a clicking noise with my tongue as I look her up and down. "Well, you're too hot to let all this go to waste," I say with a wink, and I swear she blushes just a tiny bit, giving me the perfect idea.

We walk out into the main room and I see that Rhett and Elias are back in the sitting room, Damian is absent, and Gray's standing outside one of the rooms, motioning for Landyn. I press a kiss to his lips, thanking him for being there for me during my tattoo and walk back to the other guys. They each try to sneak looks at my back or try to trick me into telling them, but I hold strong.

The guys finish up and come back to the sitting room, then Elias goes to the counter to pay for all the tattoos. When I tried to argue he just said something about angel money, whatever the hell that means. The other men start walking out to the SUV, and I sit in the waiting room as Elias finishes paying. As he does, I dig through my purse, grabbing the small stack of red sticky notes I keep in there and jot a note down on one, then press it firmly to the *Love Blooms* book and leave it in the corner of the sitting area. *A little gift to Dahlia*, I think with a smile.

Landyn rushes home, talking about wanting to rip my shirt off to see how sexy my tattoo looks, and I'm bouncing with nervous energy, hoping they love it as much as I do. The perfect tribute to the men that helped me find the light in my darkness. Men that share much of the same darkness I possess, just in different ways. Men that I know have captured my entire heart, *forever*.

Elias throws me over his shoulder, carrying me up the flights of stairs to my apartment, and I laugh the whole way up as I kick my legs against him. "Juniper!" I yell out, between gasps of laughter. "Send the flying dildo monkeys!"

Tears stream down my face as I hear a door open and multiple dildos come flying from all directions, smacking Elias in the face, arms, and chest. One of them even smacks my ass, causing Elias to almost drop me as laughter overtakes him.

"What the fuck is happening?" he growls, swatting at the flying phallic objects.

"Just a little dildo magic." I grin widely as he sets me down.

When we get into my apartment, I pull my shirt off and show them my new tattoo, dedicated to them and myself. Their growls of pleasure and possession are all that I need. I even get my wish of being fucked from behind by each of my men as they roughly pull my hair back, showing off the tattoo with two large, black angel wings, griffin talon marks, and two silhouettes of a meerkat and a fennec fox--branding them as forever mine.

Out of Darkness
Cometh Light

Calluna Tattoo Painting done by Janet Bingham Rose

Did you like Lars and Reg as much as my other readers?
Click here to see Fangs Bear'd, by first fully MM novella!
Keep reading for info from the next Spell Library book, Dahlia!

DAHLIA BY TABITHA BARRET

Little girls are supposed to draw pictures of rainbows and unicorns, so when I started drawing monsters in the shadows, people acted as if something was wrong with me. They didn't know I could predict the future. As I got older, I adapted and became a tattoo artist who gave helpful advice to skeptics.

Unfortunately, my abilities have caused other kinds of problems, especially when it came to romance. Can you imagine meeting a fun, handsome guy who seems interested in you but instead of envisioning yourself having a good time with him, you can only see how things will end? Breakups are worst, especially when you never got to the good parts. That's why I refuse to date anymore.

Now, I feel like everything is about to change. I keep drawing the same symbol over and over again. Is it a warning or it is a sign of something good headed my way? I'm not sure, but I'm positive that it involves the intriguing men I've just met.

Dahlia is an Adult RH Paranormal Romance / Fantasy Romance in the Silver Springs shared universe.

Keep reading for chapter 1 fo Dahlia or click here to read today!

CHAPTER 1

DAHLIA BY TABITHA BARRETT

"No matter where you are, I will find you!"

I held my breath when I heard the voice echoing through the air. I tried in vain to keep my hands from shaking, but it was useless. Trapped inside the fog, I had no idea where I was or how to escape.

The cold mist settled on my bare arms, chilling me even more. I leaned against the freezing marble wall behind me and tried to figure out which direction the voice was coming from. If he was behind me, I would run straight. If he were in front of me, I would find the end of the wall and run past it.

"You think you can hide but you're wrong. I'm stronger than you are. Just come out and stop wasting my time!"

I closed my eyes and felt the tears pooling as my fear skyrocketed. The voice was all around me. How was I supposed to figure out which way to go?

If only I had a weapon or a large stick, something useful, I could at least defend myself.

Desperate, I reached through the fog and patted what

felt like grass and dirt. At least I knew I was outside. That gave me more options.

When I came up empty, I cursed myself for not letting my father teach me martial arts or birdcalls, something useful that would help me fight or summon help.

"Just come to me and I'll go easy on you. I promise."

I rolled my eyes at his mocking tone. He had no intention of letting me go. I didn't know what he wanted, but I wasn't stupid enough to believe I would live through this experience.

I wanted to yell at him or threaten him, but the fog was messing with my head and disorienting me. If only I knew where I was, I could form some kind of plan of attack. I couldn't see the ground, so running without twisting my ankle or falling down like one of those actresses in the horror movies who was too stupid to leave the house once the killer showed up was out of the question. Instead, I could keep the wall to my back and let it guide me somewhere.

I stood up and kept my hand on the wall. As I walked, I felt bumps and ridges as if an image was carved into it, though I couldn't see anything.

I kept a steady pace and finally found where the wall ended. Walking around the side, I realized that the wall wrapped around so it probably was a building. My heart leapt at the possibility of finding a door. Maybe I could hide inside.

When I found something that felt like a door handle, I tugged and tugged, but it wouldn't open. Damn it! Think, Dahlia! How do you get out of this?

"I'm losing patience, which means I will hurt inflict more pain for each second you delay the inevitable." The voice sounded like it was right behind me, but I still couldn't see anything.

Maybe he couldn't see me through the fog either and he expected me to freak out and scream, giving away my position.

Staying silent, I tried the door again, and thankfully, it opened. When I stepped inside, the fog was so thick I couldn't tell if I was in a house, an office building or a bus station. I listened for the voice, but I couldn't hear anything. I took a deep breath and walked further into the room, holding my hand in front of me in case I bumped into something.

Sniffling as a tear rolled down my cheek, I caught the scent of damp earth and moss, which was strange since I was inside a structure.

I tried to calm my racing heart so that I could listen for footsteps. I gulped when I heard something scraping the ground next to me. Squinting through the fog, I saw something move.

"Please let that be a rat." I bit my lip and reached for my glasses, which weren't on my face. Dang.

The scraping got louder and my skin crawled. Something was definitely in here with me, and it was bigger than a rat.

Squinting into the fog, I jumped when a figure formed before my eyes. A corpse wearing a yellow sundress that matched her blonde hair raised her broken hand to point at me.

Without thinking, I jumped away from the corpse and screamed. I realized too late that I had let out the loudest scream of my life. I covered my mouth and tried not to break down into a full sob.

"There you are!" A hand grabbed my arm. His vice grip was too much to take, causing me to cry out.

"Stop! Please! What do you want?" Though I was being dragged, I still couldn't see who was threatening me.

I felt a breath against my ear. "I want everything you have to offer me."

I tried to struggle, but I couldn't break free. I looked up into his face to put a name to my attacker, but it was hidden behind the fog.

"Well, what the fuck happened after that, Dahlia? If I had a nightmare like that, I would demand some answers. I would try to go back into the dream and kick that guy's ass." Charlie threw her rag down on the bar and scrubbed off the dried beer.

"I woke up when I rolled off the bed and hit the floor. This is the fifth time I've had that dream and I still can't see the asshole's face. Trust me, I've tried to go back into the dream to find him, but I can't. When I do have the dream again, I can't control it. You know how you can sometimes tell you're in a dream and bend the dream to your will? I can't do it. What's the point of having a dream where you can't see or do anything?" I flicked a stale peanut across the bar and sighed.

If you liked Calluna, you'll love these other Spell Library books:

Violet by Mia Harlan

Juniper by Eva Delaney

Lupine by Hanleigh Bradley

Calluna by Jewels Arthur

Dahlia by Tabitha Barret

Willow by Elena Gray

Tiger Lily by May Dawson

Sage by J.E. Cluney

Iris by Aspen Black

Buttercup by Helen Scott

Magnolia by Melissa Adams

Jasmine by Crystal North

Join the Spell Library fan club for exclusive advanced access to books, plus weekly giveaways and games.

Want to receive news about Silver Springs? Subscribe to the Silver Springs Herald!

TO THE READER:

Thank you so much for reading! I would appreciate a review if you can.
Reviews are an indie author's lifeblood. Plus, it gives me the incentive to keep writing the sexy and swoons! I hope you enjoyed Calluna as much as I did.
Keep an eye out for a surprise novella coming soon!

ALSO BY JEWELS ARTHUR

Infernally Mine (Infernal Blade Series Book 1)

Infernally Marked (Infernal Blade Series Book 0.5)

Dreaming of Death

Twisted Rejection Anthology

Rose (Jewels Café Series Book 12)

Rose: Gettin Frosty (A Rose Bonus Story)

Rose: Feelin Thorny (Jewels Café Series Book 15)

Fangs: A Vampire Anthology

Fangs Bear'd (A Silver Springs MM Novella)

ABOUT THE AUTHOR

Jewels Arthur is the penname of a small-town Central Illinois author. She married her high school boyfriend in 2011 and together they had a beautiful daughter. She loves cats, books, binge watching tv, all things romantic, and video games. Lots and lots of video games.

Jewels has been obsessed with reading since she learned how. The obsession really started with the Harry Potter series and has continued into her adulthood. She and her husband are huge book nerds and have already started to pass it on to their daughter who says she wants to be an author one day.

Jewels has always enjoyed writing and remembers specifically writing a long piece of fanfiction of the movie Signs when she was a pre-teen. As an adult she decided to start creating the stories she is always dying for. Steamy and filled with love. With the help of some amazing authors, Jewels started her writing journey and is loving every minute of it.

Thank you so much for taking the time to jump into my fictional world. I hope to always keep you swooning and to always bring the steam.

FOLLOW JEWELS ARTHUR ON SOCIAL MEDIA

Facebook group:
https://www.facebook.com/groups/jewelsarthursmuttyswooners

Facebook page:
https://www.facebook.com/authorjewelsarthur

Bookbub:
https://www.bookbub.com/profile/jewels-arthur

Goodreads:
https://www.goodreads.com/author/show/19339151.Jewels_Arthur

Instagram:
https://www.instagram.com/jewels.arthur/

Twitter:
https://www.twitter.com/JewelsArthur

Newsletter:
https://bit.ly/2OWZqTo

Printed in Great Britain
by Amazon